FINALLY,

SOME GOOD NEWS

A NOVEL BY

DELICIOUS TACOS

For Courtney

What Do You Do

He was on Tinder. What do you do, she asked.

He was a secretary. His company provided data driven solutions to optimize cross platform branded content. He might have done something else but he'd spent 20 years drunk. The want ad said room for growth.

He built Powerpoints. When a client was on the phone he hit spacebar. Today, a Webex with Wentworth. The media planning agency. They represented the Clear and Clean Skin Care division of the Nonmedicated Facial Cleansers and Body Washes/ Poufs division of the Consumer Packaged Goods division of Johnson and Johnson. Wentworth was a subsidiary of UAG, which was a subsidiary of Group J, which was a subsidiary of PWW Group. PWW was a holding company based in Paris. Chartered in Ireland for tax purposes. PWW bought advertising time from television stations *en masse*. Sold it on arbitrage markets it created. The purpose of UAG and thus Wentworth was to help create demand for advertising time. PWW could then buy low and sell high. This was illegal in America. All advertising agencies were therefore subsidiaries of three conglomerates out of Europe.

The Webex was about Clear and Clean's possible cross platform branded campaign with *Ellen!* Its thesis was that J & J should buy in, even at *Ellen!*'s stratospheric-seeming 46 CPM. J & J's own market research found that teens and tweens identified with civil rights and related ideals. Engagement hadn't been this significant since Vietnam. Cementing the brand to environmental awareness and/ or social justice was correlated to a 38% uptick in urge to share branded content. Teens and tweens were tough. But you could seed brand elevation if you got to the moms while the moms still controlled CPG spend. *Ellen!* had moms.

Ellen! planned to profile a transgender teen. There were two candidates. Candy, 14, was a figure skater from Oklahoma. Sparkle, 15, a cheerleader/ poetess from Utah. Sparkle was the new face of Clear and Clean's campaign. Candy had signed with Unilever. Both CPG behemoths wanted in on trans teen anti-bullying. But Unilever's Dove line was entrenched with overweight over 25's. Plus, Sparkle was biracial. Her optics were better for *Ellen!* and frankly, Candy wasn't hot. Ice sports don't test well with Hispanics. Unilever would thus be ill-advised to match the 46 CPM *Ellen!* was asking. Even with the surge in show engagement from Ellen's newly adopted Pomeranian, Duchess. But for J & J it made sense.

Clear and Clean's flagship cleanser was a proprietary solvent derived from butane. It had been used to hose out tanker trucks that carried juice and other food grade fluids. When it had been found to cause cancer in rats this use was discontinued. R & D tried it as an upholstery cleaner and a mentholated cooling wipe for genitals and armpits. Neither tested well. They settled on a new facial product for teens. From 12 to 17 many young people develop acne. Whether they use facial cleanser or not, it arises, persists, then simply goes away. But brand affinity established at 12 drives purchase through adulthood.

There were 30 slides. He only fucked up once. The pie chart over a photo of Sparkle. Ass aloft in a strong boy's hot palm. Silky hair and pom poms flying. She was the spitting image of the star of a video he'd seen on motherless.com. *Teen Tranny Gets Rock Hard Riding Bro's Cock.* A Mexican boy with the face and body of a 14 year old girl and a narrow hairless penis with an angry curve like a scimitar bobbed on another boy's lap. She had moves. He'd been disturbed by his erection. Quickly x'd out the browser tab. He lingered a beat too long until the Regional Brand Outreach Manager impatiently cleared her throat.

It went well. His team knew *Ellen!* They'd optimized Target and Tide's co-branded *Ellen!* cross promotion of *Jane the Virgin.* It told Hispanic moms about Tide's soothing effect on neonatal skin. Tide was a viscous blue serum derived from volcanic ash. The co-branded online video segments garnered 2 million views per day. $1/10^{th}$ that of motherless.com. If J & J bit: room for growth. A career. In ten years he could run the division. Fifteen more and he could die. It's boring to talk about, he said.

Tell me

It has to do with marketing, he said.

What do you do exactly

Why do you want to know so bad

I'm rad and I deserve a guy who's rad, she said.

She did makeup for infomercials. Don't match dog pictures, he remembered. Small dogs replace a child. Big dogs replace a man. Women with dogs always die alone. She had a pit bull mix. It wore a bandana.

He messaged her "cunt." Waited for the three dots in a bubble to know she'd seen it. Unmatched her and opened motherless.com. It was his birthday. He was 39.

Nest Egg

He was reviewing his finances. He'd worked two years. Now he had six months of money.

If I get fired tomorrow and couldn't collect unemployment. Six months of the lifestyle to which I'm accustomed. About half to rent. Car payment. 30% of it's interest even though the loan is 6% interest. The car was 16 grand but I'll end up paying 29 grand if I stay on schedule. How financing works.

What do I have, he thought. The car. Some guitars. What else. My bike got stolen by the citizen offspring of undocumented whatever you call them now. Rent sixteen grand a year, shit not bolted down always stolen instantly. Like a doughnut on the beach snatched by seagulls. A laptop. An Xbox One with a used copy of *The Witcher* 3, which replaced a wife or girlfriend. 20 grand cash. 8 grand in credit card debt that had been charged off by the bank for two years now. That he'd been paying down 1% and 1% and 1% to keep Bank of America– actually *Banc* of America, their credit card division, from suing him. Garnishing wages. After paying 8 grand I owe $13,000 on a $16,000 car. If I pay a grand a month I'm out in about a year. Then hack away at the charge card. Call your creditor, Suze Orman told him. Ask to negotiate up to 50% off by offering one lump sum. They said fuck off.

Once the debt's zeroed out I'll still have the 20 grand. At that point I'll have paid 21 thousand for the car; it'll be worth 12. Other possessions clocking in at $1,100. I'll have a net worth of thirty three thousand. The median for Americans my age. Except for school and a few months here and there he'd worked since fourteen. Farmhand on a cranberry bog. House painter. Laborer scraping pipes on a ladder on a scaffolding. 90 degree heat, face by a fan with sharp blades that sucked up every fume for miles. Brain damage. Body damage. Assembly line at a candle factory. Short order cook. Door to door salesman. Telemarketer. Register at a drug store in a neighborhood filled with Soviet Bloc Jewish elderly yelling and yelling about the flyer not applying to 32 oz. vs. 48 oz. Sunsweet Prune Juice with a Hint of Lemon. Views on Hitler softening. $4.25 an hour. Minus taxes. Janitor.

When I've paid off the car it will break. Wouldn't put it past them to have a chip in it. It reads the balance from J.P. Morgan Chase. If you read that in the paper it wouldn't surprise you.

Another year and a half and the debt's gone. If no additional purchases. No new TV with a higher contrast ratio. Deeper blacks. Even though a lot of *The Witcher 3* takes place in caves. He needed a new mattress. Hips like an Irish wolfhound about to get mercy killed. Bones grinding into old springs. He needed new pants but $24.95 from H & M was fine. Who gave a fuck what he looked like anymore. He'd taken a work trip to Japan. An audition for his promotion. Selfie at the Imperial Palace. His eye bags in sunlight like a skin graft from shaved scrotums stitched together. Black people get stomped by cops but white people wake up in their 30's with a face that better be rich.

He was eligible for a 401(k). He read up. *You can retire comfortably at 65 if you start saving at 23*, said Forbes.com. *Even with a relatively low yield of 6%.* Every 401(k) he'd had earned 1%, lost 2.5% in fees. As for saving at 23: median household pre-tax income is $51,989 per year. Who saves on 40 grand net with a kid. It costs twice that for a school where gas huffing sasquatches don't commit Rwandan machete genocide. Nobody has money. Nobody gets returns. We'll all work till we're dead. Eating shit, having to smile about it.

If I was married– if my wife could work part time. Cover rent. That'd be something. But there aren't wives now.

If you'd invested back then you'd have money now, stupid, said Forbes.com. The interstitial Quote of the Day brought to you by Hewlett Packard. Hewlett Packard made printers that existed to lie about how much toner they had. So you'd have to buy more toner from Hewlett Packard. When the machine told you your half full toner was empty you were encouraged to mail the old cartridge to Hewlett Packard, for the environment. Hewlett Packard then sold it to someone else. The CEO of Hewlett Packard ran for president. No one shot her.

If I cut back I can save two grand a month. How much more do I need. He searched Windows for "calculator." It tried to sell him something. A feature of Windows 10 was you couldn't just search files. You simultaneously searched the web with Bing, which offered monetized suggestions. They sold you the machine and the machine sold you things you auto-paid every month until they became invisible. He paid for Microsoft Office every month, for iCloud every month. He paid for his car every month; when he took it in for service the man told him he couldn't check the brakes. These tires are so bald it's dangerous for me to take the wheels off. You shouldn't even be driving this car. They'd sold it to him a year ago. We offer factory spec tires: 900 parts, 400 labor. Financing was available.

He went to another web site and typed what he had and what he made and a 6% return and waited to hear how long until he could stop. The phone was ringing. The web site said 25 years. It was his birthday. He was 40.

Second Date

I want to suck your cock, she said. They were in her son's bedroom. The boy was about 12 and he was sleeping. And I want you to suck my cock, he said. But he didn't. They'd been doing coke for 90 minutes. It was cold in her house. He could feel his dick like a slimy canned mushroom.

He let her kneel down and take it out from his too tight pants and his day glo pink American Apparel underwear. There it was: a blue acorn. Her mouth was warm but there was a little coke in her spit and it made him feel like her tongue was wearing a medical glove. Listen, he said. let's wait for this bump to wear off. We can talk.

She looked up at him and made sexy eyes. It was his birthday. He was 36. There was a small party outside; unrelated. People in her room. He had a trapped chunk of coke burning into his sinus by his eyeball. They'd been impatient chopping it up with his Costco card. He needed to block one nostril, hang his head back and snort up a big full breath of air through shuddering coke snot to get the rock into his throat but he couldn't. He had to make a serious face back. Otherwise she'd feel insulted. Just let the little coke nugget abrade his flesh and bones, probably smoke through to his brain and give him a stroke. What can you do. I really like you, she said. He wanted to play Xbox.

It was his birthday but he'd had to buy the coke. Despite progress sex roles persist. The dealer came to Van Nuys in his cream colored Oldsmobile. You had to go out and sit in the car with him with the flashers on in the street. He was from Nicaragua. I've always wanted to visit Central America, he said, handing over folded cash. Don't, said the dealer. Is very bad place.

Will he sleep through this, he said softly. Yeah he takes anti anxiety medication. His cock was still out in the chilly air and she went at it again. It worked this time. Bend over– here, he told her. She put her palms on the dresser and he pulled her skirt up and her panties down. They'd met on OKCupid. She worked for the public radio station. After a minute she said I want you to get me pregnant. I want you to choke me she said, but he was already cumming. As he pulled out dripping on the dresser he saw the boy's eyes were open.

No Exit

Every morning he thought: I can't do this one more day. Often by the 5 offramp where a line of buses switching freeways made a bottleneck behind a blind curve. He'd be going fast around the bend and suddenly slow buses like a herd of elephant. Behind them an 80's Jap pickup with six extra feet of steel pipe hanging out the back. Sometimes with a red rag tied on it. Sometimes not. Drivers from lawless places.

Pipe right at eye level and once a week he almost got lanced in the face like a jousting accident. He'd read about a woman killed by a flying manhole cover. She was driving and an oil truck bumping over it set it spinning like a giant Chinese star. Through the windshield into her eyes like the Simpsons' dog with the frisbee. My luck it'd just make me uglier, he thought. Ugly blind and retarded. Then I'd step in the manhole.

It was Valentine's day. He'd dated a hooker once. Her busiest day of the year. The johns all wanted to talk. How do you have so many lonely men and 9/11 only happened once. So many lonely men yet science spent billions finding zero calorie sweeteners. Nothing on growing teenage girls in *axolotl* tanks. Billions spent to make a robot kick a soccer ball when who the fuck asked for one more soccer player. Drones controlled from a storage locker outside Vegas precisely target tables at Yemeni weddings but the killer at the joystick can't get a second date. They made a movie about Joaquin Phoenix falling in love with Siri. Hey Siri, he said. Do you want to talk to me. *I'm sorry– I don't understand that.*

The way she said "that." He could sense contempt. He thought about ramming today's Mexican truck pipe. Maybe gripping it two handed like something out of *300*, forcing it all the way through his brain. Instead he went to work. Around one he realized he forgot his lunch at home.

The Zombie Zone

Marcy Pendergrass was putting up the Halloween decorations. The one hot girl in the office. He'd been promoted but his cubicle was the same. Gray desk behind a gray wall five feet high. She held two rolls of fake police tape with cartoon letters. Do you want the Vampire Zone or the Zombie Zone, she asked.

I don't have a preference.

He'd been looking at a grid of consumer packaged goods branding executives. Now he tried not to look too hard at Marcy Pendergrass. She wore a black tennis dress to work. She'd crouched to pick up plastic spiders, to embed in webs she'd stretched outside his boss's big glass office. Right across from his cubicle. He saw her panties. The color of toothpaste. Then just pick, she said.

Vampire please.

I knew you'd pick that.

She said it sweetly. But he still thought: then why the fuck did you ask. She slid behind him to string up the tape by his printer. Got on tiptoes. Her hip grazed his arm, shifted the cloth of his dress shirt and gave him ASMR. His neck hair stood up. He hadn't been touched in three weeks. The warmth coming off her made him self conscious about his posture. Her breath made the cubicle humid. Jesus Christ, he thought, I am turning into a vampire.

You picked vampires because they're sophisticated, she said.

**

She'd caught him in the parking lot once. He was in his car with the stereo playing *Entry of the Gods into Valhalla.* It was the Otto Klemperer instrumental. Operas were ruined by the tenor. They sound like retarded men crying.

She was walking down the concrete ramp with a cardboard tray of low calorie bobas for the sales staff. She had on a gray pleated skirt like a Japanese porno. She saw his face in the open window and he got nervous. By the time she asked what is that he'd been thinking for seconds about how to pronounce *Richard Wagner.* It's German opera, he said.

Well that's surprising about you.

I think it would be surprising about anybody, sitting in a parking garage listening to this.

I wouldn't have thought you were so cultured.

I'm just waiting for the guy to pull up with my Grey Poupon, he said.

It was a mistake. Kraft-Heinz Grey Poupon was a client. The line of mustards had its own branding team. Sales were strong thanks to an iconic 80's ad campaign. But millennials lacked awareness of the condiment. Now he was thinking about work. Her hair was tied back, perfect black like the girls in the Mel Gibson *Mutiny on the Bounty.* He wanted to throw Anthony Hopkins overboard and take her to a beach and eat breadfruit.

What was breadfruit. Why is she being nice to me. What else do I not know about you, she said.

Jesus Christ, where to begin, he said. He turned the music down. I wish I could say I have nine secret kids and once killed a man. But I pretty much go to work and floss regularly.

I don't believe that.

On weekends I go to the pond and look at aquatic birds.

She was about to laugh.

Recently a belted kingfisher took up residence. An engaging bird. Lot of personality.

I'm about to turn 41 years old and I pay old prostitutes in Koreatown so someone will touch me, he thought. It got so bad I joined a global terror cell. I just want to die but suddenly I want to bury my face in your jet black cunt hairs and burrow into your hot musk like a weevil. I think that's amazing, she said. That you like birds and the opera.

I'm glad someone's amazed.

I was an Audubon Society Junior Birdwatcher. And I play the flute.

He was surprised. He'd heard a song coming from her headphones once in the break room. It was about drinking cough syrup.

Maybe we can go look at birds over lunch some time, she said. There's that sanctuary.

Oh yeah I know it, he said. I would love to. There's a breeding pair of pied-billed grebes.

I don't get to do stuff like that much anymore, she said. Since I moved in with my boyfriend.

**

What about you, he asked. Which one.

I think vampires have too much to worry about, she said. He heard her snip the tape. She grazed him again as she left his cubicle. Zombie life seems more simple.

How's Chad doing, he asked.

We broke up.

There was a bright light. For a split second everything looked like an X-ray. And he thought: oh God– they did it.

He saw the boss's glass wall. Marcy come back here, he said. She didn't hear. Her eyes just said what the fuck. He grabbed her arm and pulled her under the desk and she started to scream but then there was thunder and the building blew in. When the car alarms woke him she was gone.

Angel of the Morning

His buddy told him: try Seeking Arrangement. I put that I'm worth two million. I take them to a sushi place. But not one where the chef doesn't let you order. Middle income place; I tell them I don't have time for courtship. Too busy. With what they don't ask. I tell them before we set an allowance I have to sample the goods. Easy pussy.

Yeah but I want someone to like me.

Well what else is there. Tinder's dead. OKCupid, don't get me started. No girls at the clubs and I promise you it's from this shit. They all think they can get paid.

I'd sooner be alone, he thought.

Six months later he was at the ATM. The girl waited in the car. They'd met at the duck pond. He didn't know where else to take a date. The coots had gone. Buffleheads and wigeons moved on to summer feeding grounds. But there was a kingfisher. Snowy egrets.

Like all dates she pretended to like the birds. Except the geese, which scared her. There was a pack of them around a churro a child had dropped. When you got close they'd hiss with oddly human tongues. A big one swung its neck at her and she jumped back instead of leaning into him. A bad sign. What would I do if it bit her, he thought. Would I still have to defend her. The Canada goose is primarily an herbivore. But its serrated bill is strong enough to crush small crabs and other aquatic arthropods.

They'd talked like normal. He still tried to impress her. Had no other way to speak. Her message had said she wanted revenge on the patriarchy. Then a picture of her tits.

They sat by a jacaranda. When she said *white males* he could tell it was capitalized. She hated Michel Houellebecq. Liked Slavoj Zizek, which she'd practiced saying. Her purse was open. He saw homeopathic extracts. Yes but Zizek is just a Houellebecq character, he said. An ugly man pretending to be deep for pussy. She said what kind of arrangement are you looking for.

I want you to be nice to me, he said. I want you to act like you love me. He'd practiced too.

What does that mean.

We'll go to my apartment. You take off your clothes but you can leave your panties on. You tickle my back. Maybe whisper in my ear a little. I want intimacy. Like a lover's touch. I won't take my cock out. Sixty for the hour.

She had a hairy pussy and it smelled like oregano. She didn't take her panties off but they were mesh and her grizzly bear muff hung out the sides. Once he'd seen his mother's cunt hair emerging from dolphin shorts at the pool. It was just like that. White women. He'd put on *Daphnis et Chloe* by Ravel, remembering it being softer than it was. As she dragged nipples on his back and exhaled in his ear canal there'd be a too-bright horn ostenato, like something out of The Flintstones.

She didn't talk much. Just how am I doing. Is this OK. It was; she was good at it. In character. He could tell she was getting hot from the oregano smell but when he tried to kiss her she said no.

The next day he didn't want to hang himself. Thought: if I can get this with money, I won't have to chase it and lose.

The next girl was black. Fat, 19, her big soft belly rolling over him like a slick wet pillow. Her little girl face made him wish he owned slaves. But she got horny. Suddenly he was working. Pushing his tongue into her salty asshole thinking: does she like this. Same with the next one. Chinese. Fat too; she had a condo from her green card marriage to some Shanghai oligarch. Why do you pay for this, she said. You're so hot. He couldn't then not lift up her Hello Kitty dress; climb on top of her with the minimum foreplay allowed by law. Asking can I cum in you. For weeks he'd wake up to texts from both of them. *u up. wyd.*

But it was the oregano girl he saw again. One night she texted: want me to come tuck you in. She got on top of him. The mesh panties with the soft beard hanging out and she asked: same as last time. One extra thing, he said, and she said I won't fuck you.

No, can you talk to me. Like what, she asked. Can you say what you'd say if you loved me, he said. She made a face like he'd asked what's 17 times 23.

Power Achiever

The Monday before Halloween there were vegetables in the break room. Broccoli and baby carrots.

It was a sign. The merger had closed. The company had therefore switched insurance providers. The new insurance emphasized preventive care to cut claims. A new poster in a black frame outlined the benefits of healthy eating for productivity. *Be a Power Achiever*, it said. A smiling woman climbed Western-looking rocks next to a lens flare.

Larry, from Wisconsin, Vice President, Global Sales, was helping himself to a free Activia. The yogurt, a client, was playfully marketed to women as a stool loosener. Larry was 6′ 3", Norwood 6.5. Strawberry.

Happy Monday, Larry said. You still driving that old beater Benz?

How wouldn't I be, he thought. You saw me leave in it Friday. He'd had to sell his $15,000 Subaru that he'd paid $9,000 on, owed $11,000 on, for $7,000, to accommodate a rent increase. Take his 1979 Mercedes 300SD out from under the tarp where it had awaited Craigslist buyers he couldn't bring himself to call back. He said yes.

What kind of mileage you get with that thing?

About 30.

No way.

Yeah, the diesels are underpowered. Keeps 'em out of trouble.

It was true. The 300SD got excellent fuel mileage. Its 5 cylinder in-line diesel engine produced only 111 horsepower. It required a more cautious driving style. But the OM617.950 engine was well known among enthusiasts: the most reliable motor ever built.

Ever think about getting the one of the biodiesel conversions? See a lot of those around.

If it's hot enough you can run it on vegetable oil as is.

That so?

Yeah. Biodiesel you have to swap the hoses out. As is it'll run veg, kerosene, jet fuel– anything but gas.

Well you should get one of those stickers. I bet the girls melt.

I would get 0.0 more pussy advertising my car's fuel flexibility, he thought. A woman who cares about biodiesel has her own interior design business. Her dog is her boyfriend. Meanwhile I had anal sex on the first date with an *au pair* in that car, Larry. Low sulfur #2 diesel notwithstanding. Back when girls liked me. Maybe I will, he said.

Believe me, they love it. My daughter loves environmental stuff, said Larry. Even people just ten years older still thought you could speak to women.

Now he'd forgot what he came in the breakroom for. Diet Coke maybe. One cold one left. He took it, dutifully put four more from the cardboard flat of warm cans into the fridge. That left one half empty flat of Diet next to 3 full flats of Regular. 95% of all soda consumed in this office, in every office, was Diet Coke. Corporate ordered the same amount of everything. Maybe the merger would change that too.

Back at his desk. He typed passwords. Spreadsheets blinked open. Two monitors angled ergonomically. Top 5,000 advertisers in consumer packaged goods by annual spend. Key in-house and/ or agency decision makers for QSR mobile coupons, keyword: Hispanic. He would dial. Wait. I'd like to speak with you about data driven solutions for market leading brands.

**

He dreamed about his grandmother with the hose, mist hissing in the grass in the summertime. She turned the cool spray from the lawn to the rhododendrons and the cold water hit his bare chest and he laughed, and she laughed too. The flowers were impossibly big and bright, the bushes fifty feet tall, a hundred feet wide. Someone was touching him. A huge warm wet palm slithering up his knee, his thigh. Rough like a workman's hand. A gargling voice sniffling *help me… help me…*

Two hands on him now in the dark and a ghoul with a slimy bald head coated in red and black dust. No face. Throaty voice slurring: *I need help, I need help.*

The sprinklers were going. The front of him was soaking wet. He slid back and hit his head on the lip of the printer table. His Hewlett Packard printer/ fax combo slid down the slick slanted pressboard and into his skull with a crack. He was awake. The fax handset flopped off but mercifully emitted no howler tone. It was Larry. The ghoul was Vice President, Global Sales. The back of his bald head looked intact but he'd dragged a blood smear fifty feet up the nylon carpet behind him. Black trail through a maze of collapsed cubicle dividers.

Larry. Relax, man, he said.

Please… helppp. Larry looked up. Where his eyes had been two oozing dark holes glimmered with specks of safety glass. His lips half hanging off, jiggling like nightcrawlers. *Helllbbb me,* he snuffled.

OK man. Relax. Take a deep breath.

The sprinkler water smelled like the men's room at Fenway Park. They kept it in separate tanks, he remembered. It had sat untouched since the building was built. Larry, turn over, he said. *Helllbbb meee* snuffled Larry.

He grabbed Larry around the collarbones and got him halfway on his side. The front of Larry was gone. His black sport jacket and his broadcloth checked Oxford and his skin and his flesh– gone. What was left was bones. Red lumps. More safety glass, little cubes like diamonds, shot into the meat like cannonfire. He was scabbing over. It must have been a while. *Helllbbbbb mmmmeee.* The voice of the dead.

I'll help you, he said. I'll help you. Stay right here.

He had to uncrimp Larry's bleeding hands from his shirt to stand up. He looked out the holes where the windows were. The sky red and lightning teasing dark clouds. Buildings skeletal and black and every alarm in the Valley shrieking like a tree full of sparrows. The sprinklers hissing, the water dirty and cold. I'll help you Larry, he said.

Across from his cubicle wall where the poster urging *DETERMINATION* once hung, a fire extinguisher sat askew in its red box. He picked it up, held it, stepped back. Larry's hands grabbed for his legs again. And he said: sorry man. He swung his hips like splitting wood, brought it down on the temple again and again until the skull broke.

**

He found her in the break room. After the fifth office with a flayed corpse or twitching burned thing in agony he'd stopped looking. He was at the fridge dumping cartons of Activia into a PWW promotional tote bag. The corpses of the women had shit themselves. Activia had worked one last time.

Water, he thought. I should take water. The flats of Evian, a client, were kept in a closet in back of the break room. Co-branding efforts with Angelina Jolie's humanitarian work had dovetailed into an *Ellen!* advertorial campaign. For the first time, Evian was placed in 7-11 stores worldwide. He preferred the tap. He'd heard the plastic made you lactate.

When he swung the closet door open she was huddled by the mop bucket. Cold, wet, shaking, hugging her knees. Marcy Pendergrass.

Get up, he said. We gotta go.

Belinda

Are you surprised I'm here, said Belinda. Mexican girls don't date white boys.

Au contraire, he said, I've had every one in town but you.

Not the real ones, she said. I bet their parents spoke English.

She'd fucked her tattoo artist for three years. He was 44, married, someone snitched to the wife who then called Belinda's mother. I want you to know your daughter's a whore, she said. I'm going to tell your whole family. I'm going to go around your neighborhood, tell everybody. She did.

The tattoo artist came in her every time. She thought she couldn't get pregnant. He said he'd meet her when she got the abortion. He posted on Instagram from a bar instead. He had eight other women he was sleeping with. The wife still doesn't know.

When she finished the story he went to move her hair to kiss her. And she said: not on the first date.

I Just Keep Losing

We can fix the stove, said the landlady.

OK Gre–

AT YOUR COST

How are you going to even say that

YOU told me that YOU broke it cleaning the–

That's not what I said Maureen

Listen: to fix that stove I have to go in there, get the make and model number, call a repairman, wait for him, pay him for an estimate, wait for him to get the parts…

He didn't care about the stove. He'd brought up the stove because she'd been in the apartment yelling at him about the mold and the closet sliding door mirror, which was cracked. It had been like that for two years since the last woman he cared about, who cared about him– two years– had got drunk and dived into it like a parakeet into a window. Maybe high on coke too. She'd stayed at his house to watch his cat while his father died back East. She'd invited a girl over to party with. Some Chinese YouTube ukulele player. He'd said OK because he wanted to sniff their Lesbian sex on his sheets after but they'd just got drunk and broken everything. The father died. The cat died. She left. The landlady wanted $300 for the mirror.

He thought if he asked her to fix the stove, which just broke on its own, it would be a wash. She'd back off. She was about 120 years old and demented. But she was like Mayweather. She could keep getting hit. Nothing connected. He would pay for the mirror and he would pay for the stove too and he would pay the $500 rent increase she imposed because it was true, there was nowhere for him to go. From the south Mexicans had consumed hundreds of miles and from the east New York people had swarmed in coating the block with boutiques. The Mexicali juice stand now sold fourteen dollar hot dogs and the sidewalks teemed with junior associates on Crossfit Indian runs. The rent went up and the taxes went up and the money sucking machine got closer to redline but didn't ever seize up. Somewhere five Reptilians were building a space ark. They knew the secret date of the Yellowstone Caldera. It was the only explanation.

**

The day after he lost to the old woman he went to the gun shop. It was across from the office, next to the Flame Broiler Teriyaki Bowl. Fortunately he didn't have to park. Even the handicapped space was taken. There'd been a school shooting. We expect the president's remarks any minute, said NPR. For just a ten dollar monthly pledge you'll have your very own collectible NPR mug. I'm Cassidy Brown Schwartzman.

You took a number like a deli. His was 70. He waited by a beef jerky display. At the counter three harried clerks explained they couldn't sell the floor model of the Bushmaster AR-15, which hung dead center on the back wall. The gunman used one just like it. What was available was an AR-15 with an upper modified to fire .22LR instead of .556 rounds. Which even he knew was pointless.

They should fucking know this was going to happen, said the guy in front of him. He had red hair and a face like they'd pulled him out of a river. There's gonna be a run on AR's when you get an action like this. They ought to think ahead and order more. Hey man I'm Dusty, he said.

Good to meet you.

Hope you weren't here for the Bushmaster.

I think a handgun, he said.

What kind

Something big.

That's the spirit.

Maybe a revolver.

Well get a .357 and you can practice shooting .38 out of it, said Dusty. Much cheaper.

Cost's not a concern, he said.

Well good for you man. But if shit goes down you're gonna want more than six rounds. I'd get a sixteen round capacity.

I don't need that much of a clip, he said. I just want it not to be complicated.

Magazine, said Dusty. A woman's voice came over the loudspeaker. It said "23". He decided to buy a rope.

The Sherman Oaks Outdoorsman

The gun shop door was open but half the ceiling had collapsed. The Sherman Oaks Outdoorsman. Here too hissing sprinklers, shrieking alarms. He had to press his fingertip into his left ear and still the back of his head rang with the sound of cicadas. Shelves fallen into each other. Tile floor covered with flashlights and Rambo knives, spreadeagled *Guns & Ammo* magazines. *Soldier of Fortune* open to honeypot ads in the back for hit men, all sopping wet. Marcy still catatonic in the '79 Mercedes outside, in the handicapped space. He'd wrapped her in his picnic blanket. Strapped her in like a baby. Eased the seat all the way back so her head wouldn't stick up. He'd thought about taking another car, a 4-wheel drive. But the hallway floor tilted in and the first burned corpse he checked for keys groaned when he tried its pockets.

FUCKING GET DOWN GET DOWN GET DOWN a man was screaming. A boom went off loud enough that the fire alarm seemed like nothing. Fluorescent light bulb glass and shredded foam ceiling tile fluttered down on his face.

All right! All right! I'm not–

WHAT DO YOU WANT

He was out of adrenaline. The question was insulting. Guns, he said.

Hey man– is that you?

Another insulting question. Yeah I'm me, he thought. Behind the back counter by the deli number dispenser the top of a red head inched up. Dirty white drowned corpse face, cut up. Dusty had on a tactical hunting jacket with the tags still hanging off. He'd dragged the beef jerky display behind a cash register and half emptied it into a black duffel bag. Also with tags. There was a crunch somewhere and the walls shook and the alarm squealed and stopped. In the distance many others. But no sirens. Fancy meeting you here, said Dusty. His hands were bloody.

Dusty– are you going to kill me, he said.

No man. I thought you might be them.

Who?

I don't fuckin know.

May I uh,

Yeah, help yourself man. But I'm takin the food. And I'm takin the floor model. He put down his black shotgun, straight out of *Terminator 2*. Reached up where the mass shooter Bushmaster AR-15 hung. Plucked it off its hook, peeled off the sign that said DUE TO HIGH DEMAND, OUT OF STOCK UNTIL FURTHER NOTICE. Not too much fuckin ammo for it though.

What do you think I should take.

What do you want to accomplish.

I don't know. Shoot people.

Well get a bag and go nuts man, but your issue is gonna be ammo. This place was always understocked. Even before that fuckin AARP guy went ISIS.

He'd read the guy was government, but why argue. Either was plausible.

In the end Dusty helped him. Mostly. He got a nice nickelplated Smith and Wesson .357 revolver. A mean black rifle with a scope. A .45 with magazine as recommended. Dusty showed him how they worked. Bows, arrows made to slice wild boars' arteries. A .22 because Dusty was jealous over the other ammo. Got to leave me some, he said. Nice enough smile but his hand back on the gun. 22 won't do much, said Dusty, but he remembered Speed Racer killing a moose with one in a movie. Based on a true story. When his bag was almost too heavy he made to leave. Where you gonna go, said Dusty.

Don't know.

Anyone else in that building make it?

… just me.

Well good luck out there homie, said Dusty, and they hung quiet for a second like they should add each other on Facebook.

**

Marcy was still in the car, thank God. He had to smash the Flame Broiler Teriyaki Bowl's glass sliding door with a jack handle. The gas main had ruptured and the customers and cashiers burned alive, still smoking along with the griddle top beef and broccoli. A little blue flame still whispering on the end of the metal hose by the stove. In the pantry past the restroom where EMPLOYEES MUST WASH HANDS were 5 gallon buckets of vegetable oil, as he'd hoped. He made one last trip for a jar of fortune cookies, the only nonrefrigerated food. The first aid kit under the manager's desk. When he got back in the driver's seat she was conscious.

Where are you taking me, she said.

Out of LA. He started the car.

What happened in there.

They're dead. Can you trust me for a minute and keep your head down please, he said.

Why–

Just for a minute he said, and pulled out. OK you can sit up. Let me help you.

Up the street he stopped next to a fire hydrant; water oozing out around the bolts in the cracked concrete, already black. Around them trees on fire. Houses collapsed, smoking. The wind picked up; a burning *LA X-Press* hooker paper blew onto the windshield with a 2 page color spread of SUCCULENT CHRISTINA. She was fat, looked 50. He had to reach around out the window to peel her off. To the south and east, smoke columns churning dark and swarming with lightning. No cars on the road but half the phone poles were down, wires snaking onto the asphalt. How to get out. He reached across her waist and cranked the plastic dial forward to raise up her seat back.

I'm sorry to be weird but I don't think we can let people see you, he said. Whatever men are left will want a car and a girl. He turned on the radio. For a full minute the Emergency Broadcast System tone played, indicating an emergency. No shit. He turned it off.

What happened, she said again. He said: nuclear holocaust.

I have to find my parents—

Where are they?

El Cerrito— they retired out here—

They're probably dead. She gasped and he said, oh my God— I'm sorry. Now she was crying. He made a mental note to behave like a human being. She didn't know. Nobody knew. He held her hand. She didn't move. It's a coordinated attack, he said. It'll be all over. We're lucky to be alive.

And where are you taking me, she said again.

We have to get to the country. Somewhere where there's water—

Well if it's everywhere what's the point—

It will only be cities, he said.

How do you know?

Because I almost made it happen.

Aswang

Don't come inside, said Maricar. She was 4′ 11", 19, looked 14. Waray-Waray. The father a coconut farmer on Samar. There are beach there but no tourist, she explained. He'd never heard of it but decided to move there.

They were in the best hotel in Angeles. You could tell because there were so many Arabs. In the elevators they'd quietly appraise your girls and smile. One named Waleed he'd seen three times, earned enough trust to hear that your George W. Bush was a criminal. He worked for the Jews.

He thought she'd be impressed with the room but she only liked the toilet. Below off Walking Street pimps squatted on scooters by massage girls doing each other's eye shadow. They were 15, looked 12. Too young to have a license to fuck clipped on their tube tops, a photo of the fat regional health minister in a polo shirt smiling. Instead they grabbed your sleeves on the street saying *massage massage.* Stuck out a card with a cell phone number you called to get them in your room for 500 pesos. From there who knows. Maybe you got macheted.

Maricar had never been with a white man. If you went too hard she'd cry. Her cunt felt like it was wrestling him in baby oil. He pushed it in slow, pretended it was not to hurt her. It was just that he didn't want to cum too fast. When it got to be too much he tried to make himself *come inside.* So when he died he could think he might have a kid somewhere. He couldn't.

His hair was going white and he had hips like an old German shepherd but the young girls still made his cum hit the headboard. Then ten hot ropes on her belly, her neck. She pursed her lips and closed her eyes and squirmed like a baby. For a minute he just looked at her. She put her hand over her face. I shy, she said.

The shower took ten minutes to get hot and the door had a big gap at the bottom where the water got all over the room. These places had been built in a week on top of jungle, by island people who didn't understand time or straight lines. The girls had sex at 14. Ruined, they went to Angeles. Sold themselves to Koreans in loud bars. Wired the money to a hundred brothers and cousins who sat around playing cards, smoking *shabu*. They had drunk boyfriends who beat them up. A Catholic country.

Maricar showered too. She was fast. Most girls took forever. Maybe to be away from him before their time was up. Like when he'd take too long counting prune juice in the drug store basement, to get away from old Russians and their coupon disputes. *Computer won't let you? So your computer is almighty God?* She came out in a fluffy white towel and they laid on the bed, wet together. Most girls kept their distance, said *I shy*. But Maricar put her face on his chest and her palm on his belly still warm from the water. For a second he felt something. Back home girls looked at him like a worm on the street.

You're beautiful, he said.

You too, she said.

You want American boyfriend?

Maybe, she said.

Do you like me, he said.

Diri, she said, and laughed.

**

Out on Fields Avenue scooters with pigs in wire cages on the back blasted by. Hideous men with Boris Yeltsin gin blossom faces stalked from bar to bar looking at the ground. In the bars monkey faced girls danced listlessly to Katy Perry and other children's performers. If you pointed at them they'd sit with you. Sip apple flavored beer. You struggled to make them understand questions until they got bored. Back at the hotel, $40 to fuck for a minute and a half. Then just look at them. In the states these girls would have you arrested for swiping right.

Here they told you about lives on hot islands no one had heard of. Coconut orchards stretching to the white beach. Palm huts blown away by typhoons. The other men were 60. Collected pensions. Drank cheap beer in the heat until nighttime when they'd roll around in giant soft hotel beds with high school age girls out of the "escape" section of *Bridge Over the River Kwai*. They were the unhappiest people he'd ever seen. It was monsoon season. Between rains he'd see their eyes in puddles like his own death.

**

You use condom, she said. No, he said. I don't like. Please, she said.

Do you have something?

I no have a sick. But they give us talk at the bar. Health minister. *It is important to use a condom every time you have sex.* She sounded startlingly like a health minister. He made a mental note never to patronize The Drill Shack again.

Listen, I don't have anything he said. I won't come inside. Thinking how am I 8,000 miles away having this same argument. She had a tattoo that said *Malibog.*

Please, she said.

No.

She looked like she was about to cry. What's the fuckin big deal, he said. We won't fuck.

Mama san get mad.

Why?

She give you back money.

Wait– is that an option?

I go back, she give back money, very mad.

I won't make you go back.

I don't want to walk home, she said. I am a scared. At night is Aswang.

What?

I don't know how you say in English. Some girl disappear.

Instead they watched cartoons. She was 21. From Palawan. He looked at her while she slept and decided to move there. She sent money to her father who'd lost his hotel job. There are beach but no tourist now, she said. Abu Sayyaf had stormed a resort with speedboats. Beheaded a Canadian. The State Department issued a warning. The Aswang was a vampire. In the daytime you couldn't tell unless you looked into its eyes. Your reflection was a different person. At night it grew wings to hunt.

**

At 3AM someone grabbed his T shirt sleeve. He was walking past an alley; overhead a sign with Garfield promising whores. *Massage massage*. She looked like his ex's junior high school portrait. The one that got away. How old are you, he said.

Nineteen.

I can't.

If you don't like you get massage from my sister.

Behind her the sister leaned on a dumpster, made up in raccoon eyes. She was his ex's fifth grade portrait. Her hips hadn't come in. She pouted, licked her lips.

Nineteen huh? You have family?

Yes, she said, one baby. You want to see? She pulled out her phone. The boy was half white. Had his eyes.

Who takes care of him?

My father, but he is alcoholic.

And your mother?

She has mentally ill. You want massage, 500.

I can't honey, he said. I gotta go.

Wait, she said. You have both, 800. He paused. Down the street monsoon clouds miles high. Something black flapped across the moon.

Festival of Savings

He dreamed he was walking. Looked down and his hands were holding papers. Folders of mistakes he'd made. It was the day of his annual review. In one or more areas he had not been Very Satisfactory. He woke up thinking he was late. Then remembered. There had been a nuclear holocaust.

Thank God, he thought.

Then felt bad. Millions dead. Millions more burned. Irradiated. Trapped even now, lungs half crushed choking on smoke. Pinned in flaming rubble. Can't even scream, and if they did– who would come.

Still. It felt like a snow day.

They were in the car. The front seats of the 1979 Mercedes 300SD reclined fully. If you removed the headrests they lined up with the back seats. Formed beds. The Germans thought of everything. Marcy asleep on the passenger side. Really she ought to have taken the seat with the steering wheel, at five foot five. But she'd had a rough day. Sex roles persist.

They hadn't made it far. Trees in the roads. Phone poles but no live wires. He dropped a stop sign across two downed cables to see if it would spark. No light, no cracking sound. Just shrieking black winds, car alarms slowly drowning into dead battery moans. It rained. This is good, he told her. Less fallout. He had no idea if it was true. When the sun seemed to go down behind staticky black clouds the headlights picked out shapes like huge dark demons running. Outside the car you couldn't see your hands in front of you. They pulled over in a lean-to formed by a collapsed billboard. It said your partner might be lying about HIV.

The sun was rising now. He reached back, pulled an Activia from the tote bag in the back seat. Strawberry banana. Realized he'd forgotten utensils. Peeled back the top and raised the 8 oz. cup to drink it. But the product was made to hold its shape pleasingly in a spoon. The yogurt flopped out around his mouth in a gelid hunk. Ran chilly down his neck. Billions of probiotic organisms died in open air. Marcy moved. She turned toward him. Black dust smears around her nostrils, mouth and eyes. Where are we, she said.

We're still in Sherman Oaks.

Why am I in a car with you.

We're the only two who lived. There was a bomb.

That's right– you *wanted* this–

I didn't. I didn't do it.

But you *wanted to*.

I don't know anything Marcy. I don't even know if it was the same people. I shouldn't have said anything–

You *killed everybody!*

I fucking TOLD YOU I didn't go through with it. If you don't believe me, you can get out of the car and you can FUCKING DIE too.

When he yelled she got scared. That too felt good for a second.

Why, she said...

I–

Why do you have pink stuff on your face.

It's Activia.

... are you trying to shit?

No, it's... it was the only food in the office.

You didn't take the broccoli?

I didn't.

We need to get food, she said. We need to find people.

**

The Safeway shared a parking lot with a Pet Smart and a Chinese massage spa where he'd once tried to get a handjob on his lunch break. The woman was 50, pink terrycloth track suit with silver letters across the ass spelling JUICY. Police come, she explained. Massage only. He looked it up after. Three sheriff's deputies had been masturbated. Their masseurs deported. *District Attorney Takes Down Human Trafficking Ring*. She ran for senate. The election would have been next week.

They were parked on a hill. He'd insisted they look first. He had binoculars in the trunk, next to his paperback of *Birds of Los Angeles*. On the back cover a Western scrub jay and Bullock's oriole perched together by the Hollywood sign. Below, the Safeway was smoke black, glass blown in but largely intact. And in the parking lot, among the ash-streaked cars: people. Living people. Maybe 20, 30. A big white sheet with a red cross crudely painted on hung in front of the corral of pumpkins. Some stood guard. Others waited in line at a jagged hole that had been the Safeway door. A group went in, three at a time.

You were right, he said. I didn't think it would be like this. He held out the binoculars so she could see. I'm still not gonna stay here, he said. I'll drop you off. He couldn't keep a hitch out of his voice. Like he was fourteen. For a long moment she looked.

Something's wrong, she said.

What.

Why is it only men.

It's not.

Look. She handed back the binoculars.

She was right. Women and children in line but only men at the door. Men by the ersatz first aid tent. Men keeping the line orderly. Maybe we're back to gender roles, he said. Maybe the women are safer inside.

It's not like that, she said.

Well we need food, he said. There's medicine. I'll take a gun. I'll go down around the back and look. If it's OK I'll come out front and wave. I'm going to leave you the keys. If I don't come back, take the car.

He waited for her to say no, I'm coming with you. There weren't even crickets.

**

No one was guarding the back of the Safeway. He was able to hoist himself up on the concrete loading dock. Duck through a half open rolling steel door. Collapsed pallets of Lucky Charms scattering blue moons, purple horseshoes in the darkness. .45 tucked in back of his pants, as seen on TV. Past half charred towers of Angel Soft Family Paks double doors led into the retail space. A man was yelling inside. Echoing in the quiet without electrical hum. He held his breath and put his eye to the door crack.

He saw a giant naked man in a hockey mask. Back hair coated with sweat, rank even over the smell of the meat. In front of him on a waist high display of pumpkin pie filling cans a young girl bent over, naked and sobbing. The floor tiles slick and red. Ten men in a circle stood guard with machetes, axes, Bushmaster AR-15's, cackling. Heads and limbs of men, boys and old women hacked up and kicked into piles at the feet of shelves still half stocked with bags of Fun Size Snickers bars. Kneeling by the guards were the young girls who'd lived. Some weeping, others with dead empty eyes. A dark eyed man stroked a girl's cheek with a spiny king crab leg.

The fat man pumped at the girl furiously. It had been his voice through the doors. He bellowed LIVIN' THE DREAM, BABY! Looked around for approval. In the mask his blue eye caught the door crack. Stopped.

He ran backwards. Slipped on scattered Lucky Charms. Hit his arm hard on the polished concrete but pulled the pistol out as he staggered back up. The doors thundered open and the naked fat man stood laughing, his cock quivering and blood red. The gun wouldn't go off. Just like in his dreams. The safety was on. The others' eyes on him now. Some raising rifles. He scrambled back under the cargo door, hit the asphalt hard with his knees and palms, sprinted what felt like miles to the back of the Pet Smart with the wind howling. The fire exit hung open and he ducked in and slammed the door shut and waited.

Waited.

Nothing.

They hadn't chased him. Why would they. What could he do.

**

The animals were dead except one yellow-crowned green parrot, which he let out of its cage. He thought it might hesitate. Like in poems. But it flew out like a bullet through a ceiling hole. In the Amazon they ranged by the hundreds. Covered miles and miles seeking fruit. He'd seen them on vacation. In LA escaped captives had lived long enough to form wild flocks. Maybe it had a shot.

When he stumbled back up the hill with the bags Marcy was still there. We gotta go, he said.

What did you get?

Dog food. Antibiotics. Water dechlorinator– if we find swimming pools– Marcy, we have to get out of here. They were… He caught himself crying. They were–

I know, she said.

The Fisherman's Daughter

In Puerto Princesa the guard at the resort gate had an M16 with the blacking worn off. A kind smile. He made 50 cents an hour and they posted him by the road. When Abu Sayyaf took you they approached from the beach. They drove speedboats up the coast from the south; he'd read about it. If they came the guard would have to hear the disturbance 200 yards away. Run to the beach, fight off five men with AK-47s by himself. 50 cents an hour. That's assuming the boats weren't already halfway back to Basilan where they kept the video equipment dry for the beheading. The hotel came at a significant discount but the desk girl still charged him for an upgrade. We need it sir, she said. No more Westerners now because of the terrorist. She had studied hospitality. Hoped to work in California. You'd be like a movie star there, he said. The men will go crazy for you.

Her laugh was perfect. It didn't quite accept his premise but didn't make him feel stupid for trying. I don't know about that, sir.

You would have many men fighting over you. *Malibog*, he almost said, but didn't know what it meant in the Palawan dialect, or which Palawan dialect she spoke. In Tagalog it was "horny." In Visayan "riled up", which was what he meant. Many men, he said instead, which seemed worse. He was blushing.

Thank you sir, she said. If you need something I am Joy.

In his room white lizards looked back from the ceiling. He masturbated to Joy on their wedding night. Giving her their first child of many. Her eyes full of totally benevolent love. He was almost asleep when the lizards started screaming.

**

The next night, when he came back from the underground river tour, she was at the desk again. It was teak, modeled after a Polynesian ship. Do you like the river, she asked. Yes, he had; he had seen cave swallows. Some kind of wild jungle turkey digging a hollow for its nest. Unusual terns on the sheer black cliffs. No Palawan cockatoos but he'd startled a monitor lizard trying to snap a butterfly with his phone. It was bigger than him, lumbered off shaking its head. Its bite could kill a water buffalo. Its saliva evolved over eons to cultivate flesh eating bacteria. A horrible death. Yes, beautiful, many birds, he said. He was studying a pamphlet of hotel services. Her eyes were too gentle to look at.

You have in-room massages here?

Yes, she said. I give. He suddenly got nervous.

It is OK, she said. I have a license, I am training–

Oh no, it's good that it's you.

Maybe you are shy sir?

Yes, he said. I guess so. He felt if she touched him she'd become unclean. But can I get one?

Yes, when?

Now?

She laughed again. You take a shower, in 30 minutes I come.

**

When she put her palm on his neck to apply lavender he felt like he was dissolving. She'd changed into a white uniform. Like she'd just won a high school karate tournament. Her ponytail tickled his back as she worked. She hummed and murmured. You have big muscles, sir, she said.

Thank you.

Back home, sir, what do you do for work.

Suddenly he was awake. *Motherfucker*, he thought. Even in the jungle. I uh, work in an office.

What kind of office.

It's… marketing.

Marketing sir?

Yes, people who want to sell… products, we give them data.

Data.

You know what this is? Data?

You have information.

Yes. We give information to people who want to sell things.

Good money, she said. Your wife is happy, sir. Her hands slipped down his spine and she began rolling back the top of his underwear. Her hair tickled his legs and he was at peace again. I don't have a wife, he said.

No wife, no baby?

No baby. You?

No baby, she said. Not yet. Girlfriend?

No girlfriend.

Her palm on top of his ass crack made his blood change direction. What kind of information, she said.

We have every kind. We buy everything you put in your computer. Your phone, everything from your credit card. We know everything about people and we put it together so… you know what ads are?

Yes sir.

We put it together so people can make better ads.

Do you like it?

I hate it.

Then why do you do it?

I need money. Where I live everyone has to work.

Mmm… I am working until I find a husband.

California husband?

Maybe if I am very lucky. Please turn over, sir.

He was hard but she didn't seem to panic. Her fingers moved over his chest and the lizards squeaked on the ceiling. They are called "toko," she said. Later he read they were endangered. Her face got close as she plied his collarbones and her breath was cool on his neck. So do you know things about everyone sir, she said.

Yes, we look at everybody.

Even the powerful men? The government and the movie stars?

I guess so. But it doesn't matter, we collect– we have everything on everybody but we have to give it to another place before we look at it. Make it anonymous. A credit bureau. Do you know this, credit bureau? Equifax?

No sir.

You're lucky.

You can't look because it is the law?

Yes.

And you don't break the law sir? Just to find out?

I mean– who cares, I don't... who cares what some guy buys with his credit card.

You really don't like it, she said. But I think you are strong to work hard at something you don't like. The men here are not like this, sir. I think you will be a good husband, good father. When you are ready.

She looked in his eyes. He put his palm on her cheek, moved it to bring her face close to kiss him. Slid his other hand on her knee where she crouched, moved it up her thigh, warm under the white fabric. She laughed. A laugh that didn't make him feel like an asshole for trying. Shifted away from him and made wrinkles in the comforter. It is not that kind of massage, sir.

I'm sorry–

It is OK, sir. I like you too. But if you want to know me like this, sir, you will first come to meet my father.

Wait, really?

Yes, he is near here. He is a fisherman.

Is he going to kill me for touching you?

Oh no, she said. I think you will like him sir. He is always asking to bring him a man like you.

Ghost Wedding

At night a burning star arced across the black sky to the north. Past the mountains. They were in what was once a back yard. Cinder block walls around the pool still half intact. Everything up high was gone but in the dips between the hills buildings still stood. Air mostly still and cold but once in a while a shrieking hot wind would spin the dead leaves, send them clattering against the concrete. It carried burned magazines. Excel printouts, emails marked HIGH IMPORTANCE. The pages spiraled around and hissed against the walls in the dark.

She'd been nervous about having a fire but there were still fires everywhere. The pool had a black sun cover; the water was clean and warm. They'd washed up and he'd looked away while she was naked. Checked the rashes on his arms. So far they hadn't been sick. The star rose up fast and something else bright fell off it and twirled in a spiral; plummeted down somewhere to the east. They're still launching, he said.

Why?

I don't know, maybe the system just takes over.

Will they hit here again?

Maybe.

Can we eat something?

They had Activia. The fortune cookies. Half a case of Slim Jims and some Sunkist cans they'd found in the greasy black rubble of a Shell station. The charred cardboard Slim Jim case still had part of a sentence that ended: BRO CODE. He handed her three Original Flavors. Thought the words "Snap Into It" but didn't say it. The pool furniture was burned so they sat Indian style on the concrete around the crackling palette wood. Flames so hot the nails were glowing. I can't get the plastic off, she said.

Here– they make these fucking things–

The crenellated end of the Slim Jim plastic had a cut stamped in where you were supposed to tear it open. It had never worked once. He'd been eating Slim Jims for 35 years. He bit the ends off and handed the sticks back to her. Spitting out the plastic he could taste the grain the cattle ate. Salt warm around his tongue like the ocean. Oh my God it's good, she said.

I know right?

She laughed. I hated these things before.

They're a guy thing.

I wish we had a whole truck full of them now.

These might be the last ones there will ever be.

What he meant was the last time the cattle would hear their brothers screaming as they died. The last time a 20 year old out of Chiapas would walk out bleary eyed at sunrise after unpaid overtime. Five bucks an hour under whirling razor blades that made him deaf, hacking at bloody tendons twelve hours a night. Steam from boiling meat vats a mile wide burning his eyes, some convict up the line talking shit about stabbing him over a Spades game. Coming out at sunrise just as his wife left for her own shit job, swimming in reek down to his bones but *used to it*. The last machine that rolled the collected suffering of these living beings into a stiff brown stick that that made your breath stink. Popularized as a gas station impulse buy by Macho Man Randy Savage barking ART THOU BORED at children suffering existential ennui. Co-branded with the Tabasco line of sauces as part of a *brand elevation* campaign, along with Tabasco's line of short sleeved button down shirts embodying the keyword *zesty*. XXXL the best seller– and you couldn't even open the fucking package– he looked up and she was crying.

My mom is dead, she said.

I'm sorry–

My mama

I'm so sorry–

She took care of me when– when I got hurt. She held my hand. She would talk to me when he left me. I was 29 years old– she held my hand like a little girl– my dad

I'm sorry.

They're all gone, my sister, oh my God, my sister…

Suddenly he remembered his mother's hair and he was crying too. I'm alone, I'm alone, she was saying, and he reached over his camo compound bow and razor tipped feral hog arrows and held on to her palm and she let him. They cried for a long time. When they were done, she said Chad, too. That fucking asshole.

What happened.

He left me, she said. He left me because I said to quit his job.

What did he do.

He was gonna be rich, she said. He was gonna be rich and I didn't care. He worked for a bank. He did acquisitions.

An *M & A guy*, he said.

She looked annoyed. Yes– he was. He talked people into selling their companies. He had a guy who was, like, a metallurgist. What he was working on was big. Chad took him on trips. They went to Vietnam– I think he cheated on me. We went skiing together. He was a genius. He made a new alloy, it was going to make bridges that didn't collapse. The way you made it, something about the process– there was less pollution.

Oh wow, he said.

Chad was going to sell it to Gillette. They found out it made razor blades go dull faster. I told him to quit and he didn't want to leave before the deal. And he said you don't understand. If I don't do it will be someone else. If we leave I'll be a *nobody*. He meant like me. Like you– but I don't want him to be *dead*.

She paused. What about you.

I had a mother. My dad was dead– it's embarrassing–

Tell me.

I was alone already. I was sad before this. What I had to lose I lost already. I was a fucking failure.

Don't say that–

I lived alone with my cat and a dog killed him. And I fucking had to apologize to my neighbors for abusing the dog after. My therapist told me. I do want them to be dead. I should have crucified that dog. I was trying to be a better person. It was a fucking mistake.

Did you have anything you loved?

I wrote, as a hobby. I wrote stories.

Were they published?

He laughed. Only interest I got was a rich guy who wanted me to write his OKCupid profile.

Did you?

Yeah. He met his wife from it. She was beautiful. A *software guy*.

Did you like what you wrote?

Good question.

She was quiet for a second. Tell me a story, she said.

He thought. Realized he had one. But when he looked up there was a man climbing over the wall with a gun in his hand.

**

He was standing with a hog arrow drawn back. The bow's pull was smooth. It would add, he thought, at least +1 to attack and damage rolls. The man wore little glasses, had a salt and pepper beard. Bluejeans. Improbably he wore a polo shirt with Tabasco bottles on it. They were dancing with golf balls. The man was raising his revolver.

DON'T DO IT MAN, he said. He lined up the razor arrow tip with a hot sauce bottle. What do you want.

You guys have food, the man said. His eyes dipped to Marcy.

We can't help you man.

I don't mean any harm.

The fuck you don't. Get the fuck out of here.

I just want to talk man. Please– but he kept looking at Marcy. Kept looking.

Are you fucking kidding me? You're not taking her. Get out.

You got one shot with that bow man, I got six. I just want to talk.

He let go. His aim was off but the man started to scream. It turned into a sound like hot liquid pouring in a paper cup. His gun arm was limp and his other was flailing at the arrow shaft, planted in the top of his chest, to the left. Up to the fletching. Behind him on the cinder blocks a fat blood splatter. The arrowhead had pierced bone flesh and sinew, as advertised. The gun was on the ground. The man sat down. Just staring ahead.

You shouldn't have come here man.

The man just stared and gurgled.

Marcy can you bring the bag.

What?

Can you please bring me the bag with the medicine, he said.

The man was half conscious as he unscrewed the arrowhead and pulled the shaft back out through hot blood. His eyes rolled back as he felt it. Marcy brought the bag. Listen to me he said. LISTEN– he grabbed the man's chin. Waited for his eyes. Held up the jar of Fish Mox Forte Tropical Aquarium Amoxicillin. Shook out a handful of caps and dropped them in the Tabasco shirt pocket. TAKE THESE. TAKE THESE EVERY DAY.

He put down an Evian and an Activia. If I see you again I'll kill you, he said.

**

They moved the tent to a back yard up the block. Agreed to sleep in shifts. The car might have been safer but it was easier to spot. He offered her the sleeping bag but she liked the blankets. It took a long while for him to calm down.

You were great today, she said. Thank you.

We have to get to Angeles Crest, he said. Away from people. Can't trust anybody.

I know, she said. Are you OK?

One thing is bothering me.

What?

Tabasco branding with golf. Affluent males over 40 don't– didn't– drive household condiments.

It boosts casual fine dining use, she said. The guy goes to Applebee's and asks for Tabasco.

Oh shit, you're right.

We don't have to think about that stuff anymore, she said.

Thank God.

What was the story you were going to tell me.

Well it's not mine, he said. But I read this thing in the New Yorker. About this old Chinese woman in Brooklyn who got scammed out of her life savings. This woman had a son who was sick. These people, other Chinese people, came up saying they knew a witch doctor. They said her son was in grave danger. He was suffering under a curse.

Go on.

To get rid of the curse the witch doctor had to take all the woman's possessions and bless them. So she gave him all her cash and fine China and you know the rest. These women don't call the cops because they feel too stupid. But what got me was the curse. It was from a ghost. The ghost wanted the son for a husband.

Holy shit.

Yeah. The son had a ghost attached to him. And this is common. Ghosts who die alone just wander in this netherworld, latching onto people. Chewing at their souls. Because the ghosts are lonely. Back in the old days, when this happened, they'd have a ghost wedding.

Really?

Yeah. You married a girl ghost to a boy ghost and they could be together in the afterlife. They'd be happy. But in modern times, the Cultural Revolution, they tried to wipe the traditions out. People forgot how to help the ghosts. So these angry, lonely, doomed ghosts just wander around lost. Fucking things up forever.

She rolled over a little. Leaned close to him. He could feel her breath on his neck as she got close. You know what, she said.

Yes?

I'm hungry again.

You want a fortune cookie?

Yeah.

He unscrewed the jar and handed her one. Took one for himself. Opened the clear plastic pouch and broke the cookie. Put half in his mouth, warm and crisp and sweet. Squinted at the little white paper. Pink letters. It said the greatest danger could be your stupidity.

Talk to Her for Me

On his 37th birthday he got an email. I love your OKCupid blogs, it said. Would you write my profile. Some messages. $500. Vlad.

He didn't write for money. Instead he made cold calls for a real estate office in Rancho Cucamonga. I see the lease is almost up on your refrigerated warehouse. There's a new property with rail spur. Specifically designed for meat storage, or citrus. If you meet your wife I get ten grand, he said. He was kidding, but Vlad said: done.

Vlad already had a profile. He was handsome. Had money. Said it was from software. The new way of saying your dad. Lived near the beach. Had a law degree. There was no reason Vlad had to hire someone to write OKCupid messages. Write OKCupid messages at all. But women like to be chased.

You seem like you must do OK, he said. Not that I don't want the work. But why are you asking.

I don't get the real girls, said Vlad. I get the girls who want a free house so they can think about astrology. You seem like you get the real girls.

Are you OK on a date?

I can close, said Vlad.

He got to work. What to say. I'm eight feet tall, he typed. Ten billion dollars. Nineteen inch penis. I'll choke you if you want.

I promise to make you like me. Leave you twisting in the wind. Erased it.

When he had something he sent it to Vlad and Vlad said here's my password, just post it. Let me know when you line one up.

**

Her name was Brie. Vietnamese. I want to go out with you, he said. How about it.

Forward of you. Tell me about yourself.

What is there to know. I'm one of God's creatures. No more significant than an insect, but no less perfect.

Does that yacht belong to you?

We just call them "boats."

Not to be rude but you seem like an asshole.

I'm a product of our civilization.

I've dated "software people" before. You're either assholes or autistic. And you don't seem autistic.

Thank you. Anyway I want to go out with you. How about it.

Tell me a story, she said. Then maybe.

**

When he started the story he was trying to be a dick. What women want. But she told him: don't be like that. It's not who you are.

He started again. A little fairy tale. A man hated his life and took a magic drug to forget it. Tell me another, she said. He fell in love with a sex toy who became a real woman. She died. Another. He married a whore but she murdered him. He fell in love again but tried to be nice. In her bones a woman's purpose is to propagate evil. Another. He turned into an old man and died alone but a unicorn saved him. He got a job and married a nice girl and was eaten by a vampire. There was a magic bird. It died alone too. All ridiculous. But it was about how he was afraid. She was afraid too, she said. The world was a trap. Whatever you try just makes it worse. We're doomed. All of us alone. She understood.

Finally he told a story about the end of the world. In the story he fell in love. When he got there he almost cried. Because that was the most unlikely part. I love this, she said. I love everything about this. I want to go out with you, he said. How about it. She said yes.

**

The next morning he got a text from Vlad. A thumbs up emoji. And a new OKCupid message. Hey, she said.

Hey.

Can't text at work. Long story. I had a wonderful time with you.

I get that a lot.

You're different than I thought.

How so

More to the point. Your dick is bigger too, lol

He felt something shift in his chest. Like an old box falling from a high closet shelf, full of pictures of the dead. Paused for a minute. I have to tell you something.

Oh my God, I knew it. You're not really separated–

No– actually I don't know, maybe. But it wasn't him, he said.

What do you mean

It was me. I'm a different guy. He hired me to write to you.

Holy shit

I'm sorry to bring this up. I'm sorry I did it. But there's something about you. I really like you and I'm sorry. Can you forgive me, he said. Can we talk about it.

It was a day before he heard back. Whoever you are, she said, you're amazing.

Thank you.

Can I ask you something?

Yes?

Can you keep writing for him?

Father of the Sword

Joy had the day off. She came in the morning. Took him to the beach where her canoe was waiting. Do you know how to drive one, she said. It is traditional Philippines boat. PVC pipe bolted to the sides on struts to make a catamaran. Black nylon fishing net heaped in the aluminum hull.

It was high tide. White sand stretched out into swaying weeds under calm water. Out on a pier a Chinese family studied distant ships with binoculars. The only other tourists. Tall storm clouds pulled sluggishly at the horizon. The night before he'd taken the scooter into Puerto Princesa to find sunscreen. A hundred kinds but only one that didn't bleach your skin, for tourists. In a separate area of the pharmacy. On the boulevard by a harbor full of shipwrecks kids dancing in school uniforms stopped him for pictures, laughing. He woke up early. Spent long minutes smearing sunscreen on. Toweling it off. He didn't want his nose red but didn't want to be shiny either. Appraised his gut in the mirror. Sitting down like it would be in the boat.

She sat in front, golden like a part of the sunshine. He waded out up to his knees pushing the boat out. Lost a flip flop in the sand and she laughed. We are going south, she said. My father is not far from here.

He did know how to drive it. He'd gone canoeing on a family vacation, at fourteen. Kept his boat next to his cousin's; she was sixteen with big pink sunburn tits wet in a white one piece and he thought about them seven miles downriver. Little hard on in his trunks keeping his belly warm. She was a grandmother now. He paddled south past the resorts to where the mangroves began. Families waded chest high in the salt flats gathering clams in their basketball shirts. They grinned and waved. Fish with zebra stripes chased one another in the sunlight. Are you sure he'll like me, he said.

Yes! Don't be afraid, sir. He likes Westerners. He has worked on ships, traveled many places. He is a scholarly man.

OK.

Before this, where did you go in Philippines, sir.

Manila.

Anywhere else?

… Pampanga.

You mean Angeles? All the men are going there. For the girls.

I was visiting a friend, he said. He told me there are vampires there. *Aswang.*

Yes sir, here too. Some people say at night they hear them flying. But I have not seen it personally.

Up the shore the green wall of the mangroves broke into a lagoon. Steer there, she said. Inside a pool shaded by leaves. Children playing tag in the water. Girls on boys' shoulders splashing. When they saw him they went nuts. Tom Cruise! they screamed, pointing. Donald Trump!

Rodrigo Duterte! he said pointing back, and they laughed. To the right the mangroves formed a channel. Older kids stalked the tall arches in the roots. Pulled out crabs in nets, their claws frantic in the air. It is not far sir, she said. Around a bend, a cave made from the hissing trees. Huts and houses on the muddy shore. Three little canoes like theirs pulled up on the sand. One long mean-looking speedboat, four engines askance on the back, props in the water. *TABAK* painted on the side with a crude cutlass in a bronze fist.

Men on the shore, mending fish nets, hacking at bamboo shafts with machetes. Women weaving hut walls out of palm leaves. A screaming rooster tied to a tree with twine and a water buffalo with clay covered skin, a neck like a dinosaur. But no dogs. Welcome to my home, she said. A wiry man chopping at a bamboo pole looked up, put his machete down and ran into the big house. He finds my father.

**

When the door clicked closed behind him he saw the guns. Battered AKs leaning on dirty wallpaper. He heard his heart suddenly. Knew he would die. Relax, said the old man. You are a guest.

A concrete house. Palawan didn't get typhoons but it was the only way they knew to build. In the entry a big table, mismatched office chairs, papers. A laptop. Paintings of old boxers, like everywhere here. Outside the chicken burbled, worried. The old man had kind eyes. Maybe five foot two. As he approached the boat to help Joy out to shore he'd cast an appraising eye. Made a muscle pose. You brought me Arnold Schwarzenegger, he'd said. Too many consonants for his tongue.

Inside he gestured to sit. Murmured something to Joy in dialect. Telling her go somewhere for tea. She obeyed.

You are afraid of our guns, he said. They are necessary here. For many years, trouble.

Are you–

Am I ISIS? I am a Muslim, sir. But all people are my brothers and sisters. We are in your country too. The *states*.

Yes sir. California.

And you are here for tourism.

That's right

Where have you seen.

Manila… Pampanga

For the women.

I was visiting a friend.

A man wants a woman. It is a part of nature.

It's not why I'm here.

For what then.

He paused. The girls were near the airport that took you to the island with the rare Philippine cockatoo. He still hadn't seen it. Nature, he said.

My daughter says you don't like your work.

Why are you asking me this? Can you just tell me what you want– I'll cooperate–

I have told you, you are a guest. I will not kill you. I want to know what you want from this place.

I wanted to retire, he said. Maybe here.

Not America.

No, it's not– it's not a good place.

Why? You told her you earn five million peso–

Yes but it's not like you think. It's not *worth* as much.

Oh?

They take it from you. If you make more the rent goes up. You work hard and you do what they fucking tell you. And the women look at you like a worm.

The old man was laughing.

I mean it– I have to work to pay to work to get a woman's attention so she can reject me. Love is impossible. A house, a wife– a *second date,* impossible. Normal things. I'll never hold my first child. Those things just *ended.* Yes, I hate my work. And *I'm afraid of losing it.* They get angry if you're not *thankful* for it. That's a *bad attitude.* You have to lie every day, every minute, and say you love the thing that's killing you. It's Satanic. What do we have, better toilets? The men are all liars. The women are barely people anymore. I'm barely a person anymore. I'm starting to *like it.* I'm starting to feel proud when I *close a deal.* To sell *branded entertainment.* To sell *Verizon* to *fucking moms*– it's *all like this.* Everything exists just to sell you shit and you have to sell shit too just to live and they make you fucking *smile about it.* I'll get *old* like this. Alone. Nothing but my *career*– I wish you would kill me. Please– is that what I'm here for? To cut my head off? Trust me, no one gives a shit–

The old man laughed again. And you sell information, he said. For this job.

Yes.

I know your *firm.* I have seen your *Linkedin profile.* He spoke the words like binding a demon.

OK.

We are at work on something here, he said. A project. When we are finished, perhaps things will be better.

OK–

But first we need information.

I can't–

You think I am a terrorist. But I speak to the Westerners here.
Like you. Some will not tell the truth. But they *know* it. When
the sun is covered in darkness, when the stars fall, scattering;
when the mountains are annihilated and what you possessed is
in flames, when the beasts draw together in their hordes– your
soul will know then. What you made with your life. They know.
That is terror. You know.

He did know.

When you go back, you can speak with Joy. *Via Skype.* We will
only need a little from you. And when you are finished you can
come back for her.

He waited to say yes. It took a second to sink in, that the old
man hadn't asked. Hadn't had to.

He stayed three more days. Kissing Joy under the waterfalls.
Her eyes full of love, like his dream. High in the trees the birds
cried, mostly out of sight. Just flashes of white feathers. Red
streaks like their guts were slashed. Then it was time to go. Back
to work.

The Big One

In the morning they were going to move north. It had rained again. At 1AM maybe. The water tapping hesitantly at first on the tent roof and then walls of it making rivers of ashes, crawling cold in the dirt under the nylon floor. Hissing over the dying trees and ripping the gray grass out of the mud like a cancer patient's hair coming out in clumps. Snaking into holes in the blown out Sherman Oaks roofs around them. Waking up mold spores in wrecked sectional couches and pianos and entertainment centers. Fattening up the burned out corpses of TV writers on hiatus who'd moved over the Cahuenga pass seeking highly rated schools. The scorched ribs of the pit bull mixes they'd *rescued*. It had taken months to get one. The shelters were bristling with volunteers and their alimony money. They interviewed you like Harvard. They wanted credentials. Certificates of education about rattlesnakes, coyotes. You had to try and try. You had to know somebody. Nothing left alive to soak up the sounds and the air made white noise like a jet engine next to you. She had second shift to listen for killers but when he woke up her cheek was nestled in his armpit. Her hair on his neck still wet, smelling like campfire smoke and swimming pool. The rain calmed down to a tap tap tap on a detached gutter pipe somewhere and a gray light was picking up. Her fingers on his collarbones and her eyes were opening and she was pulling down the zipper in his 25 degree rated sleeping bag and kissing him. Her mouth stank like Slim Jim debris caught between teeth for sixteen hours but he got used to it. She pulled open his cocoon and the cold air hit his belly. Slipped off her toothpaste color underwear and crawled on top of him and he felt like he was easing into a warm bath in winter. Moving slow with her hot palms on his chest and he looked in her eyes, seeing a child outside time that he wanted to hold and protect. When he came the world went white and he could see her black bones.

Industrial Society and Its Future

Marcy Pendergrass was putting up the Fourth of July decorations. The one hot girl in the office.

She made no small talk. Her heart not in it. The CEO gave a speech, remotely. You may have read about merger talks. Nothing has been determined. As you know in this competitive landscape we can and must do more with less. In the coming weeks, departments may be evaluated. I expect with your competitive drive and your love for a challenge we'll emerge from this process stronger than before. Applause over the conference room speaker phone.

The summer after freshman year of college he worked nights in a candle factory. They'd fire you for going near the trash. If they let you take broken candles you might break candles you wanted. He worked the shipping line. It was called Plymouth Rock Candle but they barely made anything there. Just assembled it. Product came from overseas. You'd open a crate and an oxblood color bug the size of a men's loafer would crawl out dying. Second shift once startled a cobra sleeping in a case of votive holders shaped like Christ. The candles were sold by women at parties. They were a loss leader. Revenue came from selling women the idea of selling candles to friends and neighbors. Seminars and training materials. The women sold women who sold women and so on.

The shipping warehouse was biblical. A million cubits high. So big there was haze in the distance. He was a temp. Third shift was an experiment. Keep working 24 hours. 9PM to 5AM he stuck UPS labels on boxes packed with Yankee Bayberry

Everflame™ Jar Style his coworkers picked from scaffolding racks that leaned over and gave you vertigo. You could feel the electricity that ran the conveyor belt in the nerves of your arms. Next to him a man pulled a lever over and over that dropped styrofoam peanuts from a hanging bag the size of a high school gym. Labels were a cake job except one or two hours a night, when a guy up the line screamed CANADA and you had to start reading the tiny address as the box rushed by. Three provinces need an extra sticker. Housewives sell each other candles in places like Yellowknife where babies die from blackflies. If he fucked up and forgot the sticker one more time one of the guys on truck said he'd kill him. He'd done 20 years for murder. Six dollars an hour.

One night Mark, the manager, called the whole warehouse to sit in a circle. They'd succeeded. So productive the company made third shift permanent. As such half of you will be let go in four weeks. Anyone talking about layoffs will be fired immediately. I know this is hard news. Also, second shift packed 5,000 unicorn votive stands with no bubble wrap. This product is genuine glass. Before we start on quota we'll take them out and repack.

Violins began to play. Management chose an adult contemporary mix. Annie Lennox's "No More I Love Yous" four times per night. Mark was watching as they scotch taped bubble wrap on the smiling cartoon unicorns and they couldn't talk about getting fired. On break he'd told the foam peanut man he was taking Amtrak to Long Island. Visiting a girl from school. They'd taken acid together. Their souls were intertwined. They'd get married. Someone had to say something while Annie Lennox overenunciated *IN SI-LENCE* so the peanut man said: hey. Did you know this guy has to go 200 miles to meet a girl. Mister New York here.

Surprised it's not the fuckin moon, said the convict.

They made fun of him all night. But he thought about her hair. Felt hope. After the layoff he moved his trip earlier. Couldn't wait. When he got off the train she introduced her new boyfriend.

**

This time he was safe. Larry, Vice President, Global Sales, overheard him talk about telemarketing. So you have cold calling experience. They moved him up to sales. He took a girl to dinner to celebrate. She got a direct deposit every month for an old man to watch her take a bath, then half fuck her with a bunched up condom on. The amount was ten times his raise. The client's money came from an instrumental role in developing the USB adapter. Half the time his dick felt like it went in upside down. On sales calls the voices felt like cigarette burns on his neck.

The office nervous. But not him. Now he was revenue, not cost, plus he planned to steal key data on government officials from the company's database. Give it to terrorists. Marcy's summer dress was white and her panties were striped like a candy cane. When she reached high to hang tiny American flags she showed 36 hours of armpit stubble. His mind became two micrometers tall and he wandered among the fat cut hairs like in a forest, feasting on her smell. He wanted to say don't be afraid. Don't be afraid to lose something we all hate. Why could I never speak to a girl like this. We're both just mammals. How am I so beneath her.

Are you doing OK, he said. And she said: we're not supposed to talk about it.

Larry left his office unlocked over lunch every day. Laptop open. He was afraid if he let his computer sleep Windows would install a software update, while he was presenting. He stuck in the USB drive. It was upside down. Had to take it out, flip it, push it back in hard before the laptop fan started whining. As instructed he left it in for a minute and then pulled it back out. Only one more step to go.

Red Dawn

The new bomb punched a hole in the sky. Over the fireball the black cloud ceiling of seething H. R. Giger demon intestines broke open. You could see blue. The blast was up high. Miles and miles East. The sound came half a minute later with heat like a blow dryer too close to your neck. Then quiet. They'd come out of the tent barefoot in the mud, lower halves naked in the cool wet air, peering over the cinder block fence and squinting. Is it safe to look, she said.

If it wasn't, we're already fucked.

Will there be radiation?

I don't think we can do anything. If we're gonna die we're gonna die. How do you feel?

I feel OK.

Me too.

Did you cum in me?

I did.

What if I get pregnant?

We'll eat it.

She laughed.

**

Since the last strike was East they went West. Neither knew the roads. Their phones used to tell them. His had still been in his pocket. She played Garage Band while they drove past caved in houses and cars, wet and slumped and coal black. She made a song with the vibraphone until the phone asking for money from a server it could no longer reach made it die. Filthy coyotes pulled at the tendons of dead children in the front yards. Scattered when the car came. He kept the revolver in his lap but it felt like it was alive and might shoot his nuts off. He held it out to her. Do you know how to use this, he said.

Do you?

Don't be an asshole.

I used to go the gun range with Chad.

So you had cool dates together.

Are you *jealous*?

Fuck… kind of.

How?

I don't know how to feel.

Me neither.

Can you just shoot any adult males you see, please. I don't trust anybody.

OK. If I miss, run them over.

I'm serious. Everyone we've seen is rapists.

I was surprised you weren't.

Well the day is young.

You're not like that, she said.

When they found the freeway it was just heaps of black metal. Thermonuclear war had occurred during business hours. But a minor economic uptick meant one per cent more cars on the roads, which doubled all drive times. Everything had burned and exploded. Right past the on ramp was a huge ashen hole filled with charred skeletons reaching desperately for the ledge. We have to walk, she said.

Not yet.

What are we gonna do? It will all be like this.

There are fire roads in the mountains, he said. No idea if it was true. He'd spent a thousand hours in the hills seeking woodpeckers. Never seen a fire road. But he aimed the car toward the hills at random and had a piece of good luck. The houses stopped. The pavement stopped. On the leeward side from the city there was sage and green grass from the rain. Dirt that hadn't been on fire.

Oh my God, she said. Pull over.

A dirty creek ran down a slash in the hillside and green vines grew with white and purple flowers. Bees and hummingbirds floated over them. He cut the engine in the old black Benz and it rattled for half a minute more sucking diesel out. He'd have to start using the canola oil soon. He hoped it worked. It did on *Mythbusters*. Wild peas, she said.

She climbed out of the car and squatted by the bank where the water ran into a pipe under the road. Picked some and brought them back to him, with one little flower. A fabaceous herb, she said. Look– five petals. The banner, the wings and the keel.

This is amazing– you know about plants?

Yeah, I love botany.

Is there anything else we can eat in these hills?

No.

Well shit.

I'm shocked this is even here. They're poisonous. If you eat too many they'll paralyze you.

Jesus Christ–

It's OK. There's not enough to hurt us.

He took one. It was stringy and made his teeth hurt but it tasted like fresh cut grass smelled. Everything tasted like life itself now. Like the Earth. A rattlesnake looked on from the mud. He could swear it blinked. When he went for the rifle it was gone.

**

They came around a bend and there it was. A water tank high up in tall grass. Sides aluminum colored instead of black. Hills high enough and far enough outside town that things were sheltered. You could still read the signs. One of them said FIRE ROAD. I told you, he thought. A pipe ran down from it and it had leaked and tall black mustard weeds sprouted yellow flowers.

I can't believe it, she said.

It's the best thing I've ever seen.

They parked the car and he took the Evian bottles to fill. I'm going to look for more peas, she said.

Don't go too far. She shot him a look like *you're not my boss.*

Take a gun.

It will be fine.

I don't want to lose you.

You barely know me, she said. But she took the revolver. Walked off into the ravines.

He took a long cool drink straight from the leaky pipe before starting on the bottles. Maybe twenty minutes before he heard six loud fast cracks echoing. Ran to the car. Guns half spilling out the black duffle bag and he grabbed the one close to his hands, the rifle with the scope and the black stock and the pointy .308 bullets long as his thumb. Tried to slam the bolt home while he was running and couldn't. Had to stop. It was sticky, fucking up somehow– finally after what felt like a ten episode miniseries he got it. Checked the safety. Red means dead. Fucking remember this time. Ran again until her head popped up over the grass and the chaparral and she was laughing. GET ON THE GROUND, GET ON THE FUCKING GROUND, he was screaming, and she was laughing and saying it's OK, it's OK. A man stood in blue track pants and white sneakers and a hoodie that said WHARTON.

It's OK, she said. He had the gun at his shoulder but the scope just looked like opening your eyes underwater. The tiny bright dot with crosshairs seemed to appear and disappear at random. He couldn't make WHARTON appear in it. You're gonna miss, said the man. And you're gonna scope yourself. You'll lose an eye. It's OK, said Marcy.

What happened.

I startled her. Honest mistake.

Is it true?

Yes, she said. He's nice–

Don't feel bad. She missed too.

He lowered the gun. Are you OK, he said to Marcy, and she said yes I've been telling you. My name's Kent, said the man. And he pronounced the *T* too hard as he reached out a hand from his hoodie pouch pocket.

Kent was white. Maybe 45. Maybe five foot ten. His hair was black with a stately amount of gray at the temples. His face was like a senator from Utah. He sounded like a commercial for paying to make sure your loved ones were taken care of after the unthinkable.

You came up from LA? Said Kent.

Yes, Sherman Oaks– sorry, I didn't mean to–

Not looking too good down there I bet.

They're raping people.

How's the infrastructure.

What?

The roads–

They weren't great to begin with. Where did you come from–

Calabasas. We got hit hard too, and they keep coming. But if you came up here for the bunker I'm in it.

He looked at Marcy, then at Kent, then at Marcy.

You don't know about the bunker, said Kent.

Is there food?

Enough for me to wait it out for a while, said Kent. But not too long.

Anyone else with you?

Just me, said Kent. Would you like to take a look?

I should lock the car.

We'll wait, said Kent.

**

He came back with the .45 in his belt. Red means dead. Kent and Marcy had started walking and he had to jog to catch up. Over the ridgeline was a barbed wire fence on a concrete slab with a heart that said CUNT painted on it. A path through a hole in it. Nestled in the hills old blown out cement buildings. City buses picked clean. Everything spraypainted with *Fuck Piss Cunt*. Down a staircase cut in the hillside a giant concrete platform. Thick looking steel double doors in it, maybe forty feet long. For the missile crew, said Kent. Steel, dirt and concrete. We've had air blasts so far but if we get a ground hit there'll be fallout. This was made to take it. Do you know what this place was?

No–

This was a Nike site. Military installation for missile defense. They built fifteen or so of these around the city, to intercept atomic weapons and aircraft–

Fucking great job–

Well it's been defunct since the 70's. But it wasn't to protect people. They protected military assets. Ultimately it was more efficient to just move them away from population centers where the nukes would hit. I was an Air Force man myself.

By the missile doors was a small square hatch and Kent crouched down and opened it. The hinges screamed and the sound bounced around a tunnel underneath and startled sparrows out of the creosote bushes. A tiny steel ladder dropped down a chute into blackness.

Kent brushed the rust off his hands. I'm glad you're here, he said. I don't know when they're coming but they will be. The Russians, the Chinese– the Arabs. We're going to resist. They want to take this country, they can pry it from my cold, dead hands. Come take a look and we'll talk, said Kent. He gestured at the ladder. You go ahead.

There was something about the air. Not a smell but something cold he could feel in his lungs. He hesitated. Then held his breath and climbed down into the dark.

Evaluation

He needed a raise. To save enough money to quit. HR was six months behind on his annual evaluation. This meant they knew he'd ask.

He'd had to follow up. The meeting was this morning. 9AM. The HR head would review his evaluation. They'd have budgeted an amount. But they wouldn't mention money unless he asked. They'd pass his request to some anonymous personage. Come back with a smaller amount. A prior evaluation noted he did not always dress for the job he wanted. He would need to wear his crisp white shirt. It was custom tailored at Men's Wearhouse. A client. He'd had to buy it for a wedding. All cotton. No armpit stains.

He'd got up at five to iron it. Hung it on the shower curtain rod in the hope the shower steam might soften it. It didn't. He had to spritz it down with the water gun from the iron. He took care to rinse out the chamber three times in case the old water had rust. Laid the shirt on the carpet and laid the iron on it and nothing happened. He waited for the iron to get hot. Tried again. This time it hissed. The fabric got marginally smoother. He spritzed it again. Ironed it again. It was still wrinkled. This was one section of one side of the sleeve. The whole shirt was spread out on the floor. It looked like there was a schooner sail worth of gesso white fabric left to go. He dragged the iron on the shirt intently. The correct speed took many tries to calibrate. Slow enough to flatten the shirt but fast enough to not leave iron shaped burns.

When he was done he took the tupperware of chili he'd packed the night before. And the wet smooth shirt. Not folded. Not on him. The seatbelt and his back against the car seat would mangle it into a state far worse than when he'd started. Carefully draped the long unfolded shirt over the back seat. When he got to work he parked. Carefully hoisted the shirt up and out. Carefully slipped it on. It was hard to chicken wing his left arm into the sleeve with the right arm in, without wrinkling the shirt. Hard to bring his hands to chest level to button the cuff buttons. Even this movement left an accordion of deep folds at the inner elbows. He bent his body only where this area was already ruined. Closed the car door. Locked the car. Picked up the heavy tupperware and his briefcase off the trunk lid. When he got to the dark glass door from parking garage to office, he put the briefcase down. Then the tupperware. Pulled the door open. Held it with his foot while he picked up the tupperware. The briefcase.

The meeting was nine o'clock. Later he would heat his chili. Take it to the park. Sit on the bleachers by the baseball diamond. Eat in the sun watching starlings and squirrels. A celebration. At 9:10 he got an email. We have to delay until this afternoon. Apologies.

The bleachers might be dirty. Instead he microwaved his chili. Ate in the break room. The florescent lights sputtered. Made a sound like Tuvan throat singing. He opened the tupperware. Steam twirled out. The edges of the chili were molten. Bubbling. He dipped in his white plastic spoon. Held it aloft. Regarded it.

An amoeba-shaped hunk of meat squatted in the red grease in the spoon. It formed a face. Frowned malevolently. *You know what I'm going to do you,* it said. *To that fucking shirt.*

He did know. He paused. He blew on the chili in the spoon. Hand shaking slightly. It rippled in the hot liquid like distant tyrannosaur footsteps in *Jurassic Park*. He waited. Waited. The searing meat hunk glowered. *You think I won't get you, faggot.* It was ninety nine per cent cow and one per cent the thumb of a man from Chiapas. He'd walked miles in the dark desert under the Milky Way. Forests of dry branches, hooked spines crawling with scorpions. To work the blades overnight at the meat packing plant. What he'd loved was playing his *requinto*. He'd been due for a raise too.

Go ahead, pussy. You' can't wait forever. His hand shaking like he was reaching out to get it cut off and he stretched out his lips and the meat sensed its moment and jumped. He shifted back fast. Caught it on his black pants and his other hand instead. The soft place between his finger and thumb burned like a hornet sting. That's right bitch, he said.

The Youth

They were on Skype. Hello baby, said Joy.

Hello beautiful

She was in her hotel uniform. White polo shirt with purple piping. Hair tied back. He could picture the big teak desk in front of her. Feel the jungle air like the bathroom after a shower. Did you do it, she said.

Yes.

OK there is only one more thing. You will get a text with an address. You need to take the drive there.

OK, then maybe–

Yes, baby. After. Bring it to Four Finger Fritz. Her mouth fought to not put vowels between the letters. Four Finger Fritz. It is very important.

And then I'll come–

OK baby I have a guest, she said, and she made a kissy face and her fingers got impossibly huge and he was back on the home screen. Hold music.

The destination was outside Inglewood. A scrapyard. Look for the white Winnebago outside. He went on a Saturday. The hills above Burbank were on fire and the air smelled like Burn-In-Bag Match Lite charcoal smoke all the way down the 110. A client. Ty Pennington hosted cable segments on grilling targeted to dads and dads at heart. Co-branded with a gel men over 50 could rub on their thighs. They said it increased testosterone.

It was a hundred fifteen degrees. The sidewalks sprawling with pup tents and blanket forts and the buildings were plumbing parts stores that had steel cages pulled down over windows spray painted TAMIKA GOT A FAT PUSSY. He parked the black 1979 Mercedes SD with the blistering roof paint in front of a party store with a donkey pinata hanging. The side facing the window bleached white like the bones of an old fish on the beach. A skeleton with skin like pork rinds blew its way around the tents and stacks of bike frames in a black electric wheelchair. Cinder block shaped head cocked out wildly at a Stephen Hawking angle. Wrinkly loose eyelids stuttering. A barefoot man in wet yellow silk shorts ambled by with a 1987 boombox on his shoulder playing Run DMC. Another man built like Kimbo Slice speeding up the street on a 23 inch pink girl's Huffy bicycle jumped off it at full speed. He began beating Yellow Shorts as the bike caromed into the gutter. The boom box shattered on the street with a sound like a thundercrack. The origin of the dispute was unclear.

The Winnebago was the kind with the orange and white trailer bolted on an 80's Toyota pickup truck. The front wheel by the curb was off and the truck sat on a jack that made you want to kick it. Rusty brake caliper dangling like a bear trap. Someone had spray painted the windshield. Road cone orange letters:

CHINKER PUSSY = SIDEWAYS

-    RUPI KAUR

It was true.

There was a door on the side. He knocked. It opened out. A face.

It was *him.*

The boy with the public radio mom he'd fucked on coke five years ago. He'd be seventeen but he looked like a man. Forty. His head grown gigantic. A bristly blonde beard with no mustache and where his hand gripped the aluminum doorknob his knuckles looked like bags of molars. His ring finger was missing. His black T shirt had death metal calligraphy you couldn't read. A succubus. The boy squinted for a second. Holy shit, he said.

You recognize me?

I think you fucked my mom.

I did, I'm sorry–

Hate to break it to you bro– you weren't the first. You're the guy from Philippines?

I guess.

Come on in.

Inside, the trailer was trimmed in fake pine veneer and the floor was stacked with filthy copper pipes. Coils of old wires only shiny where the bolt cutters clipped. How you been man, said the boy.

What the fuck happened to you–

I ran away. Don't tell my mom you saw me.

We haven't spoken.

And here I thought you were a gentleman. Do you have it?

He took the thumb drive out of his pocket. Passed it to the boy, who hit the space bar on an old black Dell laptop that booted up to Windows XP. Next to it a big silver cordless phone with a fat black antenna. Toothpaste green lights stammered behind the number pad. The boy plugged in the USB. Upside down at first. Flipped it. The computer burbled. Sounds like an old ball joint creaking on a washed out dirt road. It'll take a minute to see if it takes, said the boy. You want a Monster? Fridge works.

No thanks. Dude how are you living like this–

Why, do you think it's your fault?

Kind of.

There were a hundred of you.

Well I'm still sorry–

It wasn't any of that. I left because I hated school.

I hear you.

Whole day sitting some place I didn't want to be. My mom fucked but she was a good mother. She made me do homework. If she'd been a bum like you think I would have stayed.

She posts about you on Facebook all the time. She says you're on the autism spectrum–

Yeah I saw that. Maybe she thought it'd make people care. I got tested for it once and she talked about it nonstop after. I think she thought it meant I'd be rich. It just makes girls not want to fuck me.

She's worried about you man.

Yeah well she married some guy and he moved in and just... there's one bathroom. I'd have to go in after him. The smell of a forty year old man's shit– no offense. The toilet seat was still warm with one of his old ass pubes on it. First thing in the morning. And then after that, fucking *school*, and after that fucking *homework*, and dinner with them asking how's school how's homework. Nothing else.

She cares about you.

She fucking called my science teacher about how I might do better in class. I don't even care about science. But she thought I had to. Because she had this thing about me being autistic. The teacher tried to fuck her. Anyway I bailed.

Been a while now.

Two years. I moved out and went down the street and then just kind of kept getting farther away. I ended up slinging pills with the Juggalos for a while in Hollywood. The FBI scattered that scene and I was living with a couple trannies who had me jerkin off on cams for rent. People got sick of my videos when I hit puberty so they kicked me out. I was trying to make Arizona but I got caught up in the meth scene down here. They needed a whiteboy to take the shit up to Hollywood. I told them I was German. They call me Four Finger Fritz–

He held up the hand with the stump. The end still swollen, crawling with red veins that looked warm.

How did you lose it–

Fritz laughed. Punching a guy off a moped.

You hit him that hard?

No but I took the moped and must have crashed it. I was blacked out. Some guy found the finger but it was rotten.

Fuck.

I was doing great with the 13's down here, easy money. Had a nice Mexicali girl too. But then shit went down with the Somalians.

I didn't know we had those–

Yeah they come from Maine, the government brings them there. They speak English like the Pepperidge Farm guy but they're mean as shit man. They had this shotcaller Abdullah, he was a fuckin hardcase. Came out of the military. They started moving in on 13 territory by LAX. They were beefing but then check this out– he fell in love with a 13 woman–

Wait how do you even know about the Pepperidge Farm guy–

It's on *Family Guy*. You must be old enough to know the originals–

They're a client.

A client of what? What is it you do exactly, anyway?

It's complicated. It has to do with marketing.

Like what

We gather information to help... brand elevation. Purchase intent– for brands, like, Verizon–

What does that even mean, said Fritz.

We provide data driven solutions for market leading brands– and suddenly Fritz was laughing.

What?

That's fucked, said Fritz.

**

Abdullah fell in love with Xochitl Sanchez who was fifteen years old and the sister of the 13 shot caller. The Somalis and the Salvadorans went to war. It was, Fritz said, exactly like *Romeo and Juliet.* Julio the 13 shot caller ultimately told Xochitl: stay away from that fuckin Captain Phillips lookin ass nigga. At some point she obeyed. It broke Abdullah's heart. He made peace with the 13s, which was how Fritz came to do business with him. But inside he'd gone nuts. Got into some hard shit, said Fritz. Organized shit. Do you know what Al Shabaab is?

No–

The guys you're down with, Abu Sayyaf, it's the African version.

I'm not *down with* them.

They work together. The Somalis are down with dudes in Pakistan. They got guys in the ports, they work with Filipinos on the ships. Which must answer a question you had.

Is this ISIS?

Kind of. ISIS doesn't mean anything. Mostly it's a bunch of commercial operations. Abdullah said it's just a name for the believers to work under–

… a brand.

I guess, said Fritz. How'd you get into this shit anyway?

Into what?

Blowing up the world.

I'm just giving information.

But you know what they're gonna do with it, right?

I assume get money. They have some utopian project–

They want nukes man. Your company has credit card records of every big general. Every other government big shot– they're gonna find a couple who fuck kids like the guy from Subway. It'll probably be the first two they look at. They're gonna get the targeting system. The codes. *Data driven solutions for the market leading brand.*

No way–

Yes way man. These guys know how it works. Abdullah was in the Air Force. He was an officer in the Missile Command.

They gotta be bullshitting you–

Nah man. These guys are on bath salts all day. It reminds of them of this leaf they chew back home. They got loose lips.

The phone made a sound. Then the computer. Fritz was typing suddenly. It worked, he said.

OK–

I'm gonna get fifty grand for this. Go down to Venezuela. Stay out of the cities man, they're only gonna hit where the "abominations" live. What are you getting–

Not fifty grand.

A girl huh.

… yeah

Must be some good pussy–

Hey man, are you serious about this shit?

Fritz stood up. Slid a giant rough hand on his shoulder. The ring finger stump hot on his clavicle. Don't feel bad man, he said. This is coming one way or another.

Jesus Christ. Why did you tell me?

You can't stop it now, said Fritz. And if you could, you wouldn't anyway. I mean do you look at this fucking place and think: how could I leave this behind?

He felt his heart going. A sweat coming on like he had a parasite. Are we done, he said.

Yeah man. Good luck. Hope they deliver on the girl. I don't think they'll kill you at least. These Africans on the other hand– I gotta split so they don't machete me.

Then he was twenty feet from the Winnie. Walking fast googling "FBI phone number". The phone showed five bars but he had no signal.

Blue Moon

The missile bunker was black inside. It smelled like the high school athletic cage where the assistant coach who didn't molest kids, and thus hated his job, handed out jock straps. Kent following him down on the steel ladder made sounds like a xylophone that pinged around the walls. The graffiti said *Fuck Cunt Pussy*. Kent had a mattress. It looked too big to fit in the hatch. He must have folded it. Big plastic barrels of drinking water. Boxes of flour, rice; store display racks worth of Jack Links beef jerky in Sweet & Hot, Teriyaki and Original.

Jack Links was not a client. They'd had adequate success building a campaign with in-house demographic data. Diverse 18-34's antagonized a bigfoot with summer camp style pranks, and were then dismembered. Bumpers on WWE's *Friday Night Raw* showed the cryptid driving industrial vehicles such as backhoes in a demolition derby setting. I think we got our demo locked, the National Branding Director told Larry, Vice President, Global Sales, on a conference call he'd listened to on mute. This in spite of the two Wisconsinites' rapport. The National Branding Director was perfectly polite. The women could be mean but the men had sales backgrounds. Respected taking your shot on a cold call. I don't have the genny up yet but it's a matter of time, said Kent, shining a pocket size Mag Light on food stores and first aid kits and housewares. Figuring out the air filtration. Gotta ventilate the fumes or we'll smoke ourselves before Ivan does.

You've been a busy man, Kent.

Actually I had most of this stuff in my house. Getting it here was the bitch.

Did you have family?

I might still, said Kent. Two ex wives. His hands found something in the blackness. A black rifle from the box cover of a video game.

Is that a Bushmaster?

It is, said Kent. Would prefer the original given the circumstances, but this is what I had. Thank the great state of California. The pinging sound echoing again as Marcy came down. Were you two– married, said Kent. Marcy said no. We used to work together.

**

Kent had a camp stove and had opened two cans of Dinty Moore beef stew with his Leatherman. Neither a client. The meat chunks steaming and smoldering made his guts crawl over themselves. Light from white votive candles with no ornamental casing and the blue sterno flame made their shadows stutter on the *Fuck Cunt Pussy* walls. You know what I miss the most, said Kent.

What's that.

Not steak. Not lobster. Not hot showers. I miss Chicken McNuggets. Quarter Pounders. And he laughed. Like he'd just told his grandson a knock knock joke.

That's what I miss the least– you know, I used to work there.

Oh really, said Kent, with what seemed like unnatural interest.

Yeah, I was a "senior grill crew" member– I made the Quarter Pounders.

Yes, and you trained the junior crew–

That's right, how did you know– a grill wizard yourself?

Well I was an entrepreneur after the service, you know. Aerospace. And when it came time to hire that was the first thing I looked for. Advancement in a tightly-managed environment. Someone I could mentor to succeed.

Yeah I could flip a burger, he said. Remembering like he was doing it now that the burgers were not flipped. That McDonald's patented clamshell grill technology simultaneously seared each side to perfection. He'd once slipped on mop water and perfectly seared his hand on it. The manager scotch taped a bandage on and made him work through lunch rush. That day someone left a log long as a young Burmese python lolling over the lip of the women's toilet that it was his job to clean, to perfection. You'd get one every few months.

Did you know that only ten per cent of store staff attain the "senior" designation? They spent millions developing the metrics– performance. Speed. Accuracy. They would have given you an MMPI; honesty, trustworthiness–

Is that what they teach at Hamburger University–

You're being glib but perhaps you haven't thought about building an enterprise. Providing goods and services that people want and need. An employee who won't lie, won't steal, won't cheat you out of his time. I'm telling you it's worth more than gold.

You think we'll find a McDonald's out here?

Listen, said Kent. Let me tell you a story. My old Air Force buddy Kevin was training to be an F-16 pilot. The trainees have to stock the squadron snack bar. One day Kevin headed to the operations desk for his mission takeoff. And the commanding officer said "where's the creamer." Kent paused.

Where was it–

Kevin hadn't stocked the creamer. Kevin said he'd get it later. Kevin's name was wiped off the mission board that day because if you can't trust a man with your snacks, why would you trust him with a 35 million dollar plane.

OK.

That was the most important lesson of his life. Kevin became one of the premier pilots of his time. Missions over Somalia you'll never hear about. Top Gun.

Are you Kevin?

No– you're not listening. Senior grill crew– this speaks to excellence. Your potential.

He couldn't help but feel flattered.

This is what we need. You make fun of McDonald's but *details matter.* If you didn't find your life to be such a joke you would see that this *matters.* I need people who *get the creamer.*

For what?

Because we have to organize against what's out there. We have to win. And we have to build again.

Kent, what are we building again exactly? McDonald's is fucking horseshit. And the way they *built* it– two guys made the restaurant and then some fucking salesman stole it from them. From the people that did the actual work–

And he turned it into an enterprise that made a billion people satisfied–

Jesus Christ– I'm glad it's gone–

I find your attitude so disappointing. You're throwing away the greatest lesson life has ever taught you. We need good people to make this world work again. If you're going to stay you're going to understand that I run this show. And I do things *right*–

Who said anything about staying–

Look around out there, said Kent. This place can take a bomb. This place can be *defended.* Have you had to do any killing since this tragedy?

We don't know, said Marcy. There was a guy, he shot him with an arrow but we let him go–

Marcy didn't know he'd brained Larry, Vice President, Global sales with a fire extinguisher.

So someone died in agony because you didn't have the guts to finish the job.

He might be alive–

If you think someone is living in *this* with so much as a hangnail– listen. I have *water*. I won't force you to do anything. But if you want to live you're going to work. We'll find a radio. There are people out there. The police, the military. This is the United States of America. You could be my right hand, *if* you would correct your attitude.

There was a long silence as the cubed carrots roiled in the camping pot. Almost done.

Marcy, can we talk about this alone for a minute, he said. Climbing the ladder took a very long time.

**

It was night now. The sky clear in places. A giant moon with an odd cold color leered through the clouds, huge and brilliant. It's beautiful, he said.

It's a blue moon.

I didn't know they were really blue.

Well no, this one looks blue. Which is rare– only in times of atmospheric catastrophe, like a volcano. The dust bends the red light. Or a nuclear war apparently. But it's also a *blue moon*– two full moons in one season. It's rare. "Once in a blue moon-" like a second chance.

You know about astronomy too–

Why don't you just do what he says

I can't believe you're asking me that.

I want to stay alive.

We'll be fucking fine–

No we won't. Are you kidding me? I don't like him either but he's right, we have to stay together, we have to get organized–

That's not *alive.*

What is your problem? He has food, water– he's going to have *electricity!* Why don't you *compromise*? You can stay in the tent– we can *figure it out*–

I'm not going to do this anymore. We lived, Marcy. We had a second chance. I'm not going back. I'm not going to just make shit the same as it was. And I can't fucking believe that *you would–*

I'm not leaving.

Get fucked, you dumb bitch– I should just *take* you.

Like you have the balls.

Don't test me, he said. Then knew she had. And he'd failed.

I'm staying, she said. You can go. I'm staying.

She meant it. He walked back into the hills alone. The face in the moon seemed to laugh.

Funeral

She won't come with me. She doesn't care about me. The world ended. I'm still the lesser option.

God let her have everything I want, he prayed. Let her be desired and loved. Interesting and important to somebody. Let her have happiness, let her not be alone, feel alone. Praying as he'd been taught. No one heard.

Out in the desolate hills, a mile past the water tank. Only the high passes were burned. On the lower slopes the fall grass was coming up. It had rained early.

He set up the tent. A fine product. It required no tools. He'd bought it for a trip to Montana. Saw bighorns in tall weeds in the hills outside Lincoln. Woodpeckers big as chickens. Two of them together on a collapsed pine. Man and wife. Birds always found each other.

When he heard a sound like an outboard motor on a lake he crawled on his belly to a hilltop. The sky was brown-black and full of thin clouds that moved like worms. But in the brilliant blue moon everything was lit. From here he could see the freeway. The black twisted cars. The crater. And something moving. A semi truck. No trailer. Black diesel smoke poured out the tall chrome exhaust pipes. It looked like Optimus Prime. Dirt bikes behind it screaming. Ahead a procession of tween girls naked in chains, marching, faces down. An honor guard. Brutes in masks whipping at their backs. He saw three Lord Humungus', one Reddit Unicorn, one Fluttershy. These men were dentists once. Or not even– not the jobs animals had in Richard Scarry's *Busytown.* A worm driving an apple who did something children had heard of. They were *Regional Brand Managers, Hispanic. Blockchain Business Development Account Executives. Executive* dangled in the want ads with the understanding you'd say it to women. Now they were living the dream.

It had been five days.

He watched them steer around the cars. Stop at the crater. The truck had been a bad idea. But then they could just get another one. Where were they trying to get to. The big burned hole in the ground and now what. Move up into the hills. They'd find the grass. The snow peas. The water tank.

Or maybe not. None of his business now.

With Marcy gone he could fold her blankets under his sleeping bag. Less bothered by rocks grinding in his hipbones. The hot wind made a *pfoom* sound on the nylon tent cover. At the gas station ruins where the Slim Jims were poking out from charred concrete there'd been a few magazines flapping around on the pavement. They hadn't thought to pick them up. Now he would have liked an *Us Weekly*. Something. *Inside Ashton Kutcher's $20 Million Bachelor Pad.* Stars, they're dead. Just like us.

He lay awake in the *pfoom* sound. Played with a flashlight on the ceiling. The light would make the tent visible to cannibals. But his life was over. There was nothing to steal.

**

He was in a church talking to his mother. He was saying I'm sorry and she said it's OK, it's OK. Nothing you can do now. He reached out to touch her hair and she seemed put off. It wasn't OK after all. Are you alive, he said.

Are any of us.

Do you think I did this? It's not my fault–

Everybody works, you know. Everybody suffers. You didn't have to do what you did.

Why did you send me to a fancy school and then make me clean toilets at night. Why did you make me work at McDonald's. The kids looked down on me. I had to tell them–

I wanted something better for you.

Well– I know. I'm sorry I wasted it. I'm sorry I was ungrateful–

She was gone. He'd been here a long time. Night coming on. He had to get home to his cat. Who would feed him. He needed to let him in, the coyotes were out– and he was standing with his father. Big as a bear with scars from tattoos rubbed off with a wire brush. When he was five they'd found a pigeon in the street. Stomped on but alive. His father made a splint for its wing. Kept it warm in a box of wood shavings on the porch. He would whistle to it at night until one day it flew off. He had thought it might come back to visit, but it never did.

I'll take care of him, son, his father said.

He felt an incredible relief.

But you ought to take care of someone too.

There was a sound beginning. An organ. A man in a suit. You were friends with the deceased, he asked. He looked like Tony Todd from *Candyman*.

Was he? Yes, he said. Very close.

How long?

My whole life.

You loved him?

Sometimes.

Well I think thing are about to wrap up, the man said. I'll see you outside. And there was Marcy in her toothpaste color underwear. Dirty hair, dirty face, the most beautiful girl he'd ever seen. He was asking why did you leave me. I didn't leave you, she said.

I'm sorry I gave up–

You didn't yet, she said.

I didn't want to lose you.

You're still here. But why did you let me go. It's not safe.

A hymn played. Things were indeed wrapping up. *And did those feet in ancient times walk upon England's mountains green.* He remembered it from Monty Python. And they'd sung it at his school. In *chapel.* Years later he'd looked at the lyrics in a book of hymns. *Something something dark Satanic mills.* The Industrial Revolution. From some William Blake poem. The school was kids whose grandparents had money from factories and slaves. That was who read William Blake.

There was a crowd now. He recognized every face. People murmuring, mumbling, losing their places; half-coherent lyrics swirling around big stained glass windows that were beginning to melt. Jesus with a sheep. Jesus with a U.S. Navy corpsmen circa 1912 kneeling, offering him something. Old bearded men in togas. Peter or Paul or somebody. There was some convention as to who had what face since 30 AD but he could never remember. Holding a book open to three Greek letters he couldn't read. Pointing up an impossibly long finger. Eyes of the pictures all blue. The coffin was closing. New growth pine, semigloss. He had a headrush coming on and he was walking fast up the aisle toward a back door open a crack. Everyone looking at him. A thump as the door slammed behind him. A black vestibule for a second. The big gray sky outside. Then the wind picked up. And he fought, but he was being carried.

Treehouse

There was a raft in the catfish pond and one time Bryan kissed her under it. Both of them holding onto the ropes the 55 gallon drums were tied to the old deck wood with. Hanging with their legs dangling into the cold deep water. The sunlight out past the shadow of the raft made rays in the silt that seemed to go down forever, even though it was maybe 8 feet deep. You could almost feel the slimy brown bullheads squirming in the mud. They had a stinger on their side fins that felt like frozen metal going into you. The plastic barrels making noises on the wood like bongo drums.

They were whispering. The sound carried over the water. He made her laugh and she looked up nervous at his fingers on the white nylon ropes. Water spiders big as a coffee can lid lived on top of those barrels. Came down at night to stalk the elegant silver bugs that skated on the water. And he kind of wrestled his legs around her waist in her white one piece bathing suit. Wrapped his ankles around her and pulled her in while she was laughing and sucked on her bottom lip a little. And she stuck out her tongue like she and Tanya practiced on their fists. He'd eaten a grape Otter Pop and his mouth tasted like it. And when they pulled apart his tongue still had a little bit of that color. Someone did a cannonball off the raft and the corner dipped down to where it almost hit her head and they swam out separately and didn't talk about it. Thinking about it made her arm hairs stand up after.

When school started again they started talking. He'd call her and she'd be near the phone so her mom wouldn't get it. Take the band aid color receiver on its long curly cord into her room. Sit against the door. Talk about kids in his class. Movies. Softly so her mother couldn't hear. He loved *Aliens*. She made her father rent the tape but he insisted on watching it with her. It was rated R. He'd liked it more than she had. The ecology of the creatures didn't quite make sense.

They talked so long the phone handset would stay warm after. His voice made her feel like someone was tickling her back. Why don't you come out to the treehouse Saturday, he said.

The boys had a treehouse. Even though they were too old for it now. Ricky McAllister had a car even, a hardship license. A Mercury Topaz in metallic teal. Somewhere past where the last tract houses sat half finished in the mud. White plastic sheets flapping off them that said *Dupont Tyvek*. Beer bottles everywhere and bullet holes in the old gray plywood. Cicadas screaming. We'll pick you up, he said. We're gonna get beer.

How? Does Ricky have a hardship license for that too-

His brother's home.

Ricky's brother was in the army. His fiancée was pregnant. There was a joke that no one knew what the baby would look like. She worked at the antique store. It was called *The Town Pump* and so was she.

OK– what will I tell my parents–

Tell em you're getting drunk with older boys–

I'm serious.

Tell them you're visiting Ricky's brother, helping him with his PTSD.

**

She put on her lipstick two hours before. She'd worried that riding her bike would make her sweaty. But it had rained enough to be cool. Not so much that the mud sucked in your bike tires out past where the hot top ended. God was looking out for her. She laid her bike in the tall wet weeds and waited for the Topaz to come. She was early.

In the car the boys played AC/DC so loud you couldn't talk. Her friends still listened to the Backstreet Boys. Ricky was fifteen but his fingernails looked like he worked on cars and his voice sounded like he smoked. He had blue eyes like a movie star but the whites were red. Pupils the size of a pencil dot. She was in back with Bryan and in the passenger seat in front was Ricky's cousin Steve, who had epilepsy and scars on his arms. He'd lit his shirt on fire burning garbage with an old can of gas.

They parked next to one of the gutted out half built houses. Rocks banged on the metal parts of the car underneath. The foundation full of brown water where mosquitos bred and on the cement someone had painted FUCK and SATAN. Past the last house the road turned into a dirt path into the woods. She heard great-tailed grackles whistling back in the pines. Their song was supposed to contain the seven notes of passion. On the path a female dipped dead grass into a mud puddle and flew off to add it to her nest. Steve carried the beer. Ropey muscles rippling under his scars.

Ricky asked Bryan: so is this your new girlfriend. She felt her ears get hot. Bryan said: a good friend.

You still got a broken heart for that Stacey?

Fuck Stacey.

Stacey was from the side of town with horses. She had one for dressage and one for barrel racing, and she let you know it. Sang in the choir. Her family went to church twice a week.

You wish, said Ricky, and Steve laughed.

**

The treehouse was three stories tall. It was made out of plywood covered in old walnut color deck stain. Two by fours with the ends painted red nailed into three pine trees that bled sap around the nail heads. Window holes with nothing in them. Inside, the walls had pages from porno magazines tacked up. *Oui, Swank* and *Cheri*. Women on all fours, spines bent into C shapes so their face and crotch could both regard the camera, looking surprised. Their faces looked ancient to her. The men's intent expressions made her laugh. They sat Indian style. Is this your first beer, said Ricky.

It's my third

I don't mean *today*

I've had sips of my dad's before–

But this is the first time you're feeling it.

Yes

You like it?

She did. She said so. It made her feel like she could make anyone like her.

Bryan should have told you not to wear nice clothes, these fucking trees get pitch all over the place.

They're beautiful– shortleaf pines.

I've been coming here since I was a kid. Never knew what they were.

There was a fire here, she said. A long time ago. They need it to grow. Otherwise they're outcompeted by other conifers–

Damn, Nature Channel.

Each tree has both male and female cones. See how there are different kinds? It can take a year for the female cones to be pollinated–

Haha, so they can fuck themselves–

Plants had mechanisms to prevent self-pollination, but she didn't say so. She said yes and laughed. He laughed too and it felt like she was floating. Hey Bryan come here, said Ricky.

What, said Bryan, and stood up.

You like these trees too, huh?

Yeah they're nice.

You like camping in the woods?

Yeah–

You got a sleeping bag?

Ye– Bryan started to say, and Ricky punched him underhand in the crotch, and said: not anymore. Steve started laughed like it was the funniest thing that ever was.

Bryan was twisted over panting with his shoulder pulling a *Swank* centerfold off the wall. She rubbed his back in his black flannel and felt his little muscles moving. Are you OK. I'm fine he said, I'll be fine. He does this. Relax, said Ricky. We do this shit all the time.

**

They finished the case. It felt like it took as long as a movie. She had never felt this good. Sat next to Bryan and he moved his hand to hold hers and she let him. Thought about her palm sweating. He might think it was gross but somehow she knew it was OK. They were talking about catching fish. How tourists bought fancy lures but the thing the fish liked best was just a wadded up ball of Wonder bread. Ricky, why do you hit Bryan, she said.

Because he's a fag, said Ricky. Steve laughed.

It's guy stuff, said Bryan. We forget we have a girl here. We tried to get a bunch to come but you're the only one who said yes–

You wanted to have a party?

We were gonna play spin the bottle. She felt her ears get hot again. Have you ever fucked before, said Ricky.

What?

Have you ever fucked before? It's OK if you haven't.

I haven't.

Well what about now?

She felt like she'd stood up too fast. The windows wouldn't stay straight. She looked for Bryan. He was next to her but it took a long time to find him. He was biting his lip.

I can't.

It's all right, we won't tell. The girls in our class do it. Even Stacey, she's got that college boyfriend. Plus the horses. Steve laughed.

I can't, I have to go–

Where are you gonna go? We'll get you home. Relax–

Bryan will you please take me home. I can't, he said.

Don't worry honey, said Ricky. It's fine– you need another beer? I have half left.

I have to go back–

Why did we come all the way out here then. She couldn't talk, and he said: answer me.

What?

Why did we come here and spend the whole day with you? Are you wasting my time?

No–

Are you gonna cry? Are you a baby?

No–

Why can't you just be cool then, he said.

**

Bryan went last. He wore after shave on his neck even though you could have counted his beard hairs. His eyes looked sad at first. Then he made a face like he was concentrating on a math problem. Then a sound like he was hurt, and his eyes looked like nobody was in there. An old nail was biting into her hand. Her dad would make a big deal about getting a tetanus shot.

She had to bike back home. The seat was wet and she couldn't stay on the road. When she got there she was crying. Her mother was out beating rugs with a broom and said oh My God what's wrong. And she just said I don't want to tell, I don't want to tell.

Her mother didn't push it. Just held her hand. At school they started calling her Easy Marcy. It was her birthday. She was thirteen.

What Can You Do

Hello, FBI.

Yes, I'd like to report a... a threat, it's a threat to seize nuclear weapons–

I'm sorry can you repeat that sir?

Yes, I am aware of a terrorist– it's... they're trying to get nuclear weapons, they're going to–

Can I get your name please sir?

I'd rather not say.

He was on a phone he bought at 7-11. Where he couldn't not notice the Evian rack. $35 but had full smartphone functionality. Barely a signal. Walking fast down the sidewalk and it felt like he had no knees. Vagrants sitting in zipped open pup tent doors stared him down with eyes like opossums. One looked up meaningfully as he passed. Screamed: I'm the Polish Prince of Penis.

This tipline is 100% confidential, sir.

It's fucking Ben Dover, OK? Listen, ISIS is trying to get American nukes, they're going to blow up the world–

What you're telling me sir, is that ISIS would like to have nuclear weapons. Sir, the Bureau has been aware of that–

No it's a specific plan, they have– they use a woman in the Philippines... she gives you a backrub and makes you fall in love with her, and then–

Are you referring to the MILF, sir?

No, she's 22–

The Moro Islamic Liberation front, sir

No it's Abu, fucking– ISIS is using marketing data to get nukes, I gave it to them-

You're involved in this yourself sir?

No, I– I gave them data but I didn't know what it was for, I swear.

What sort of data?

It's, they– it's credit card purchases of individuals, for, it's used for refining branded content–

And this... is going to be employed for hostile purposes?

They're going to blackmail people with it.

All right. It sounds like this is a problem related to wire transfers, is that correct?

What?

It sounds like this is a problem related to wire transfers and/or interstate commerce.

I mean I guess they have to wire money–

OK great sir, it'll be just one moment.

Then he was on hold.

**

He was on Tinder. And what do you do, she asked.

He worked in a call center. People reported national security threats. Their caller ID appeared on his monitor. He typed notes. When they finished he selected an onscreen button.

The system had three tiers. Green was credible threat. Yellow was potential threat. Red was non-credible. Drunk women reporting their boyfriends for cheating. Mentally ill or mentally challenged callers. The Fuck You Button, they called it. It has to do with counterterrorism, he said. The phone was ringing.

What exactly, she said, and he said Homeland Security, then picked up the phone and said it again.

After 9/11 the public-facing counterterrorism efforts of various agencies had merged under the rubric of the Department of Homeland Security. DHS had rerouted tiplines for the CIA and

NSA, and FBI liked to transfer their cranks in too. But mostly it was the US Post Office, Office of the Inspector General. Elderly callers. Someone tampering with their mailbox. Someone living in their mailbox. The mailbox was a demon. Oh so you're like James Bond, she said.

The phone said hello? He said yes, Homeland Security again while he typed

...Kind of...

with his thumbs. He'd thought of himself more like Felix Leiter when he pursued a career in federal law enforcement. But she wouldn't know it. James Bond was a pathetic plea for relevance from the British, who were more like George Smiley. Or not even. One of his other crusty colleagues. Whichever one was gay. Homeland Security?

How can I help you sir.

Is this a different guy?

Yes sir, it looks like you've been transferred here from FBI?

Jesus Christ, OK– I just need to report this to somebody.

If this an emergency please hang up and dial 911 for your local poli–

Who is this?

This is the Department of Homeland Security, sir. Mouse hovering over red. Mentally challenged caller.

Listen I need to report a *serious nuclear threat.* OK, he said. That sounds hot, she said. Go on.

Approximately one mile south of the Palawan Seashore Resort in a mangrove forest there's a Filipino ISIS operation. They're using a girl to get lonely guys to give them information on military officials. They're coordinating with Somali terrorists based in California to get access to American nuclear weapons. They're going to reroute them to attack major population centers. I know this because I gave them consumer credit card data tracked at the individual level–

You were involved in this, sir? he said, and typed Haha it's not that sexy. Then erased it, not wanting to say any variant of *sex* too early.

I don't want to talk about my involvement, said the crank on the phone. I need you to know that there is going to be a blackmail effort against the... against high ranking nuclear security officials.

This was credible. A shell company run by the Chinese government had recently purchased Grindr. Grindr was a smartphone app to help men have raw anal sex in toilet stalls. Idea being that the Chairman of the Joint Chiefs of Staff and/or a Federal Reserve Board Member liked to meet in mall bathrooms with 18 year old black boys. Not check ID. The idea for Tinder had been stolen from Grindr. It didn't work, because of women. U still there, she said. I'm getting bored

It has to do with national security, he typed. Mousing over Yellow. Can you tell me what kind of data you provided? Do you have a government clearance?

They don't need that– it's every credit card purchase. That sounds boring, she said. Do u like t? What is it exactly?

Jesus Christ bitch– is this fucking Linkedin? he typed, and erased it.

The elderly never dreamed that they were finding gold coins in the mailbox. That the mailbox was a beautiful nymph. As you got old your mind dried out into a thing that could only fear and suffer, he was learning. Until all you could do was yell at people on the phone.

His job had not resulted in a single arrest. Terror busts didn't come from incall business. They came from FBI agents asking mentally challenged men if they'd like to participate in terror plots. Arresting them when they said yes. He had job security. Room for growth. He earned a pension. It could start paying out in 35 years. Why won't u tell me, she said.

Never message a white woman with bright color hair, he remembered. Green means polyamorous. Pink means transsexual game designer. Blue means Type II bipolar disorder but even they can't talk about anything but your fucking job. What if this guy's right. Well how could I leave all this behind.

All right thank you for the call sir, he said. Please be assured that DHS takes these reports seriously, and your claims will be fully investigated. He went to unmatch the caller and hit the Fuck You Button on the girl before he realized he was turned around.

**

I did the right thing. What are the odds they find me. Whatever– I called them. I reported it. I used a burner phone. What will they get me for– corporate espionage?

I have to go back to work

I have to go back to work.

There's a merger but I won't even get fired.

Maybe they'll hire another cute girl. So every pig in the office doesn't have to get horny for poor Marcy fucking Pendergrass.

He had a dream about a dying seal in a black ocean with his mother's face. At 4AM he woke up when his computer speakers blasted a Windows notification. Cheerful chimes. A mandatory update had auto-installed. It had enhanced opportunities to make in-app purchases with one click. Erased his Documents folder. His unfinished book.

He searched for support live chat. Waited for the chat window. Typed. Your fucking mandatory update erased my files–

Agent–

Live agent–

LIVE AGENT

Did you mean: *I'd like to purchase a new Surface Pro*, it said.

Hyper Elite Disrupter

In the morning he fished around in his trunk. He'd remembered something.

The now filthy tent tarp covered everything. It was twisted around his old maps and tire jack and half empty 10w40 motor oil bottles. Finally he got it clear. A package of athletic socks from his mother. A genuine Nike product. Red, white and blue in a distorted argyle pattern meant to look "technological". The label said: *Hyper Elite Disrupter*.

His toes were swollen like tree fungus. Smelled like a mildewy basement. The snug new fabric felt like his feet were being dried with a young Japanese maiden's hair.

**

He parked the car on the road by the old fence that said CUNT. Climbed up through the spindly black mustard until he could see the concrete platform with the rust color bunker doors over the hilltop. Concrete stairs down the hill. An old rail made of rusty pipes. He walked slowly. Half crouched. It made him hear helicopters from a Vietnam war movie. He kept his hands far from his pockets. But no one was looking.

When he got to the hatch he ducked down and banged on it. The sound startled sparrows.

No one answered for a minute. Then–

WHO GOES THERE. Kent's voice, echoing up the chute.

It's me, he said. I'm opening the hatch.

The hinges sounded like a witch squealing over baby meat. Hard to see down the ladder in the dark but he could make out Kent, pointing the Bushmaster.

Hey man– I come in peace.

Kent half lowered the gun. What can I do for you, he said. He sounded like he was talking across a long swimming pool.

Marcy, are you in there?

No one here but me, said Kent.

Where did she go?

I don't owe you an explanation about anything, said Kent. We've seen what kind of person you are. You won't last out there and you wouldn't last in here.

OK man. Listen– you, and she, if you're here, have to get out of here. They're coming.

Coming? Who? Go where? "They" are wherever you're going to–

OK you don't have to come. Where's Marcy.

You're not taking anything that's in here.

It's not safe here, Kent. She's not safe.

Safer here then out there.

Let's ask her about that–

She doesn't want to see you, said Kent.

She can tell me that herself.

You better get out of here, said Kent. Before I start seeing you as a threat.

He almost said something.

Instead he paused and reflected. Prayed for an instant. Like he'd been taught. All right man, he said. Have it your way. Walked away up into the weeds.

**

He lay in the grass on the hilltop for a very long time. Just looking down. Finches burbling. Low wet paper color clouds cooling his neck with mist. Then the sun broke out. Finally the metal squealed. The hatch door flew up. Kent's head with the Mitt Romney gray at the temples inched up and up. Looking around cautiously. Like a marmot coming out of its hole in an old cartoon. Squinty eyes.

He shouldered the gun. Like Dusty told him. Pulled it just slightly away from his face until he could see a magnified head in the scope glass, shaking along with his hands. Weird light effects from the dirty lens dancing around the hair. A black shape like a sliver of moon slid around under the crosshairs. When he moved what felt like a millimeter the black slipped over his whole field of sight. Then when he got Kent's face again a bright beam was hitting it and Kent's eyes got startled and he was moving. Dropping out of view. Red means dead. He pulled. A sound like lightning hitting a house. Like a bomb going off.

His forehead was numb. The top of his nose. Like one minute after the best coke rail that ever existed. The crack still echoing in the hills as his ears began ringing. Suddenly his eye socket hurt so bad it was... it was... what was the word for it. He couldn't remember. What is this feeling. Did I shoot myself. Did the bullet come out the wrong end and hit me. Am I retarded now....*vibrating*. His eye bones were *vibrating*. Now it felt like when your foot falls asleep. There was blood in his eye and his forehead by the eyebrow felt like a strong hand was pinching it. Someone was screaming. Inner ears shrieking with Tibetan bells. He couldn't see.

When he looked up there was no one in the hatch and it was quiet except the screams. Over and over with big jagged breaths between. He smeared blood off his cheek. Pulled back on the cold gun bolt. A cartridge came flying out, just like it was supposed to. A new pointy bullet popped up and he levered up the bolt and pushed it forward and it stuck. He had to try a couple times. Finally he forced it hard and it went. He walked bowlegged to the cement steps down the hill, pointing the big black rifle at the grass in front of him, half crouched. Feeling like he had no knees. Screaming and screaming echoing up through the hatch. The finches quiet and he got to the ladder, put his shaking finger on the trigger, red means dead, pointed the gun down the chute and looked. Kent was twisted up twenty feet down with his skull gone. Scalp butterflied out with a tuft of white temple hair twitching. Blood pumping and pumping on the floor and on the *Fuck Cunt Pussy* painted walls like his brains were a wet towel being wrung out hard. He had a memory of running over a hostess Cherry Pie with his Huffy tire. He could smell it. Marcy, he said.

Oh my God–

We have to go.

You killed him–

He might make it, he said. She didn't laugh.

YOU KILLED HIM!

I wasn't gonna fight him, Marcy. The fucking... Morlocks are coming. The fat guys who rape people–

YOU KILLED HIM!

Call the cops, he said. Was he good to you?

… no

Then let's take his shit and get out of here.

Birds of the Amazon

By the time they saw the ocean even the dog food was gone. Freeways and surface streets still filled with burnt out cars and corpses. Some fresh. Others just black bones. Every one in a posture of agony. Not one relaxed skeleton.

The old Mercedes took the vegetable oil fine, as Jamie and Adam had *confirmed*. But sipping it for calories made their hair greasy. Their guts slippery. The car had sat low on the back tires with weight of the water they carried, but not now. Lighter every day.

ISIS had thoughtfully annihilated not just Los Angeles proper but the Greater Metropolitan Area. Everyone and everything was gone. Outside Carpinteria the road broke for good. Chunks of asphalt tossed on their sides and scorched. We can't get through, she said.

We'll turn around.

All the roads will be like this. We have to walk–

We should at least try.

This car is loud. People can hear it. We don't have much left to carry-

It's a shelter. It can get us to the mountains– he shut off the engine. It kept idling. Guttural cast iron clacking and a smell like a Chinese restaurant on fire. Finally it sputtered out. Silence like a cathedral. She was right.

You 're attached to it, she said.

That's not it–

You have feelings for your car.

OK I do. I bought this car for 800 dollars. Had her for ten years. I went to the mountains, the desert in this car. Through storms. She kept me safe. I brought my cat home in this car...

Her?

I'm sorry. I know it's ridiculous.

It's not.

It's hard to leave her.

I know.

He turned the key. Waited for the glow plug light to flash. Pushed the gas just as the starter turned over. You had to. It took finesse. The open throttle made the motor *whoosh* like a leaf blower. He steered to the sand by the roadside. Into the ashy flood ditch between the freeway and the frontage road. There had been a CarMax before the fire tsunamis. One collapsed billboard only half burned. A grinning lawyer could make Mexicans millionaires if only they could get badly maimed.

Dial *dos dos dos- dos dos dos dos.* The old wheel smooth under his palms. Tight turning radius for such a long luxury sedan. Old tires struggling in the sand. He shut it off. Waited while the engine grumbled, for a long time. Saying goodbye. It was his birthday. He was 42.

She helped him pile chaparral branches and tumbleweeds on the roof and the windshield and the blistered black hood. Took the sleeping bag and tent. He took the water, the sport duffle full of guns and bear arrows. Paused to pat the walnut on the dashboard.

We'll come back for her if we need to, she said. But you can let her go. She kept us safe.

She was right.

**

The beach looked almost like nothing had happened. Just a few wrecked boats with names from Jimmy Buffett lyrics beached on their sides at the high tide line. Black clouds of flies shimmering around the putrefying seafarers in their cabins. They carried their shoes. Peeled off their damp Hyper Elite Disrupters. The sand felt like a mother blowing cool on the soles of your baby feet. Ocean hissing. 100 yards past the ruins of the state volleyball nets the sand meandered under a cliff. There was chattering in the sky. Green silhouettes racing over them in a loose V formation, crying back and forth. Wings stuttering.

Parrots?

They're yellow crowned Amazons.

Invasive species–

No, it's a sign. We're going to make it. I let one out at Pet Smart. Maybe he's up there.

You believe in signs?

I saw these birds, these exact birds, at the clay lick at the headwaters of the Amazon river. They congregate at a cliff in the jungle to eat minerals that soothe their stomachs. They got here by a guy trapping them and drugging them. Stuffing them in his pants to fly them to America to sell. Most of them suffocate. And the few that live have to live in a fucking cage. But not these ones. They survived. They got out.

I forgot you went to Peru–

When I went there I wanted to die. I was 40. I was working as a secretary at a fucking branded content consultant and the kids on the jungle tour with me were 25. They were rich and from Switzerland. They'd been traveling their whole lives. They had girlfriends and 8 weeks vacation. I was an old man who lived alone with my cat. And my cat died. And you know what?

What.

I was so glad to be alive to see them. Parrots– yellow crowned, red crowned. Blue crowned macaws, chestnut-fronted–

Wow–

I know– you wouldn't believe how many species. You wouldn't believe how beautiful they were. And I was so glad I kept living. I was so glad I was 40 and there were still so many things to see for the first time. And now here they are.

That's beautiful.

It means something.

OK but the world ended. We need to eat. What do we do–

Whatever the fuck we want. We were slaves. And now we're not. If you tell me you want it, we'll go to the marina, we'll take the nicest boat, and we'll go to fucking Peru. We're going to make it.

**

When the cliffs ended there was a row of beach houses. Sheltered by the mountains that sloped right down into the sea. They weren't burned.

I told you, he said. Made for the first one. A gray Craftsman with a smiling sperm whale weathervane spinning crazily in the sea breeze. But Marcy said: Oh my God, and he stopped.

I know–

No, look–

A quarter mile ahead, behind a high piling of heaped boulders, a cream colored fortress jutted out on a man made sand peninsula. Crow-step roof ornaments echoed the high jagged ridgeline to the East, now dusted with snow. Mock-crenellated walls accented custom arched front facing windows in a facade carefully angled to optimize sweeping sea views. False minarets poked into brilliant blue sky. Hispano-Moorish arches beckoned to an airy and inviting atrium.

No way.

It is! she said. That's Ellen and Portia's Stately Moroccan Hideaway.

Ellen! had provided a video tour of the couple's $22 million faux Moroccan home. Ellen personally highlighted where her hand-selected housewares could be purchased. Staccato jokes about duvets and tea sets. She authored an accompanying photobook. It's a bold play, said Larry, Vice President, Global Sales. You think of *Ellen!* as a CPG/ QSR mom audience. But she's not only targeting the top 1% of her watch here for furniture buys– I'd say gay and childless 44+ with these 1600 dollar lamps– she's also elevating *herself* as an aspirational lifestyle brand. Climbing out of the mom ghetto into Gwyneth money. It's branding within branding. I don't know that we even have the tech to measure it– she really is a genius.

**

The stone door was hanging open. It had belonged to an Algerian madrassah. He was holding the revolver. HELLO, he said. HELLO. Nothing.

They must be on vacation, she said.

The central courtyard had a fountain, now dry, surrounded by authentic tile frescoes and California native herbs. True to the home's Moorish heritage, the tile designs were geometric so as not to present a graven image. A blue bird alighted on the fountain lip. In its beak a tiny pine cone. It glanced into the empty basin, contemplated, then hopped off and across the bricks to the shrubbery.

Look, she said.

A Western scrub jay.

Yes but look what he's doing.

Trying to get the pine nuts?

No, he's burying it! Watch–

The Western scrub jay was a passerine corvid about eight inches long. Its back blue as a tropical sea. Eyes alert. It contemplated the ground. Looked for the right spot. Dropped the pine cone on a dirt lump and held it between its toes and began hammering it into the earth. He pecked and pecked intently until the tip vanished under soft toast-colored soil.

Are they food cachers?

It's more than that. They're forest planters. The forgotten caches grow into trees. They create new ecosystems without meaning to. The pine cone will be opened up from all the fire–

We should stay here, he said.

Is it a sign?

I bet they have a nice bed. Plus I could use a shave– maybe Portia left her snatch razor.

**

The fridges were empty. Ellen's co-branded cheese plates and flatware in the cabinets but every atom of food gone. An engraved *thuya* wood door from a Berber harem led to the pantry. It squeaked when he pulled it. Heart thumping in anticipation of Ellen and Portia's organic low carb snacks. The shelves were empty. FUCK, he said.

Anything?

Nothing.

Can you fish?

Yeah but it will take time. We have to find the gear, maybe the boats–

We have to eat.

I know–

There was a *click click click click click* from upstairs.

They looked at each other wide eyed. Breathing extra quiet. His hand moved to the revolver handle. Finger on his lips. He motioned for her to hide in the pantry, and she did, and closing the naturally distressed harem door it squeaked. The sound again. *Click click click click click.*

He stalked through the sitting room past the L-shaped sectional in white calfskin. Spun around the corner with the big silver gun and tried to say something cool but just wheezed.

A honey colored teacup dog was stumping down the staircase. Worming down the steps like a slinky on her tiny legs. Dirty pink bow on her collar. Faux lion haircut growing in. She must have heard the pantry door. A sound that meant *food.*

J & J had integrated its "Sparkle" trans teen anti-bullying campaign with *Ellen!*'s segments featuring her newly-adopted Pomeranian, Duchess. Ellen pre-taped selecting and nurturing the rescue after her early life of neglect in a puppy mill. The buy was a success. Segments showed Ellen grooming Duchess. Dancing along with Sparkle's cheerleading. Per her father's Instagram, Sparkle was emotionally abused on social media for wearing nail polish while presenting as a boy. Now she and Duchess enjoyed tandem pedicures. Sparkle had to be angled carefully. Her artificial hormone breasts had grown in lopsided.

Focus groups indicated high uptick in key axes of brand affinity. Significant effect sizes in *Strongly Agree* for core questions:

> *Clear and Clean is a health and beauty brand that supports my values*

> *Cleansing with Clear and Clean is one way I can help change the world*

$(p < .02)$

Duchess paused on the landing. Cocked her little head to gaze down with wet black doll eyes, innocent and afraid and hopeful. Shivering. Her pedicure had grown out. Her nails like talons. Metallic teal polish chipped into scattered shapes like ice melting on a black lake. Her shaking made them *clickclickclickclick* on the imported fruitwood inlay.

He knew her name. He called her, and she came to him. They cooked her over driftwood. It was the best meat he ever tasted.

deliceioustacos.com

Cover: mattlawrence.net

Printed in Great Britain
by Amazon